PERSONHOOD

Thalia Field

PERSONHOOD

Thalia Field

A New Directions Book

Manufactured in the United States of America
First published as New Directions Paperbook 1497 in 2021
Design by Eileen Bellamy

Library of Congress Cataloging-in-Publication Date
Names: Field, Thalia, 1966– author.
Title: Personhood / Thalia Field.
Description: New York : New Directions Publishing Corporation, [2021] | "A New Directions book"
Identifiers: LCCN 2021003036 | ISBN 9780811229739 (paperback ; acid-free paper) | ISBN 9780811229746 (ebook)
Subjects: LCGFT: Poetry. | Essays. | Drama. | Fiction.
Classification: LCC PS3556.I398 P47 2021 | DDC 818/.5409—dc23
LC record available at https://lccn.loc.gov/2021003036

10 9 8 7 6 5 4 3 2 1

New Directions Books are published for James Laughlin
by New Directions Publishing Corporation
80 Eighth Avenue, New York 10011

The good end happily, the bad unhappily, that is what fiction means.

OSCAR WILDE

—

What else is it that should trace the insuperable line?

JEREMY BENTHAM

for the captive wild

CONTENTS

HI ADAM!

—

"A word's reach extends a speaker's grasp, or what's a language for?"
Stanley Cavell

Adam: *Hi Adam!*

Did you hear your name?

Adam: *Hi Adam!*

It's not your name. But the bird was not ashamed.

* * *

The curse of a long life: Adam lived like 930 years, Noah like 950.

"These are the generations of X"—

and God saw all creation filling the face of the earth, and lo, it was good. The non-Adam animals bore their names peacefully, but the new wife was not obedient or quiet. There was a bite, and then hiding, and lo, God's garden was ruined. He boxed up Adam and Eve and dropped them, flightless, into exile.

＊

You visit the sanctuary, the long, low-ceilinged barracks in a repurposed factory-chicken farm where there are almost a thousand "exotic" refugees. You're led to think the prison-like environment is also an ambiguous form of gift.

The cement floors have been smoothed; there are 9-gauge-steel interior enclosures, windows added, and access to outdoor pens.

You wonder how to conceive of this place: an old-age home, a foster home, a nursery, a hospital, a way-station, a final resting place, a zoo, a rehabilitation center, a place-holder, a parenthesis, a pale excuse, a last ditch, an asylum—

They stare at those who enter; some move away, some toward.
But everyone stares, waiting for time to end.
Time is unbelievably loud. Or eerily quiet.
Some have made a friend after long years of being housed together. Some cannot.
Some were never loved and don't know what they've missed, or how to connect with anyone. Most have been abandoned by their families, some once, some many times.
Some are left with a letter of explanation, apology, desperation.
All are heart-broken and dying of it; die of it.
One prefers to live under a box on the floor.
A few creep, bent over as though crushed by an absurd ceiling.
Some rush for attention; most simply pace.

Adam: *Hi Adam!*

None can move as their bodies were designed; all are crippled. There is a quarantine for new arrivals and a hospital room for inevitable injuries. Some attack their cell-mates. Some fall. Some have mutilated themselves to near death: from infection, from skin loss, from open wounds. Many are bald. Some are hideous. All are beautiful as sun on water.

2

The weird thing about the energy of sunshine: fruit must make itself open.

At first, branches and leaves hide the fruiting clusters, but the beak or hand reaching in begins to feel which are still hard and tight to the stem, and the heavier, softer ones that come off easily, fall into the palm. Then there are those too far gone, with open juices and insects already gorging. To pick at the perfect time the perfect fruit for that very day is to decide among many, to be grateful for one.

The brutality of so much sunlight unabated would beg anyone what to do with all that desire. The leaves withstand, and transfer, don't they, to the bark, the roots, the branch, the wing . . . the flight through the canopy. To fruit. Does that energy flow down into prehistoric soil, or just stay near the eyes ready to explode, as seeds do across the whole place?

Adam: *Hi Adam!*

In old-master paintings, the Garden creatures stand in a weird *contrapposto*: a tiger, a rhesus monkey, an elk, a dog, a giraffe, a large white horse gathered near a tiny pond with swans, peacocks, and a lion. A nearby rabbit and a sanguine cat. A startlingly small ox. A mouse. A heron. An elephant. A goat. No one fights or hunts. All pose in the landscape, where amazon parrots, a pair of macaws, often a cockatoo, sit in the brush-stroked trees.

Entering the sanctuary, you're shocked at the birds' sheer charisma, imbued with what is lamely called *personality*. They sit in their walk-ins, or along an archipelago of low-strung hemp islands. Peering and pinning, raising their wings or feet as you pass, in greeting, in warning, in jest, they seem alive but painted.

A voice grabs your attention from down the corridor—

Adam: *Hi Adam!*

Springtime in captivity. The first task of naming.

Streaked sunshine, a gardener, a landscape of colonized and awkwardly incongruous beasts, and two Europeans in a figurative pose. Yet none are depicted who would've truly hungered at the bounty: insects, bacteria, fungi, cankers, plagues, infestations, sterilities, plaques, gummy or sticky ooze, hardening and dead limbs, and up from the soil, the others, the fleas, the biting flies—

To imagine a paradise one must create favorable conditions for certain outcomes: scenes of unreal sympathy, and limits to what we imagine would be chaos otherwise.

In other words, only obedience gives meaning to a command—as a name does for he who names, forsaking all others—

Adam: *Hi Adam!*

A stolen egg or a stolen bird, which came first?

A stolen voice, or something to say in it?

Raised alone by a God, hand-fed and made divine through the outstretched finger, the original orphan steps up without knowing the songs or smells of his kind, or that it's ok to fall into flying. Maybe Adam never had a childhood. Born of a word and raised in amorphous fantasies of extreme specialness— maybe he never learned to find his food, who to love, or the joy of hundreds of miles of flight in a morning. He walked the garden unable to know he had wings for hands—

Belle: *Happy Birthday to YOU! Happy Birthday to YOU!* . . .

Henry: *Hi Henry!*

No individual bird exists, it could be said, individuals can't, in any life, exist without whole populations of their kind. But for parrots, pair-bonding in the flock also gives meaning and shape to a lifetime, just as for Adam, named, God grants a mate, flesh of his bone, and joy and suffering like night follows day.

Springtime in the exotic wildlife sanctuary: new growth, super-saturated colors, the preening, pungent odors, the strutting and mauling, the shrieking and chasing, attacking, brooding, hackles raised, feathers raised, slicked and pulled, the rushing back and forth along the mesh, along the perches, all eyes on the others, from perch to branch to wire to perch, pursuing with eyes first, beak open, the ruffling of the engorged throat, the twitching of tails.

The object of lust has a broom or a bucket, fights back, kicks, deflects the driving energy coming from the longer days, the rise of heat and stimulation of song—

What makes song? Does it stop short after one burst, or go on for a morning? The syrinx produces chords; an organ we don't share. Sing very fast, up to thousands of notes a minute, like a laugh. Many duets, and pair coordination, or songs entwined in spite of lonely bodies dancing to the music, finding beats and bobbing heads, feet stomping energetically—

Poppy: *Whatcha doin'? Whatcha doin'?*

Lucky: (*human laughter*)

Buddy: (*horse's neigh*)

Cookie: *Hello Cookie!*

Henry: *Hi Henry!*

Rainbow: *Rainbow!*

Someone reaches for a camera and broadcasts the infectious pleasure to YouTube; a million views! Everyone wants a clever bird like that!

Belle: *Hello Pretty Bird!*

In myth, the snake uses human speech, a loan from the devil. He uses fruit to point out what it costs to become domestic, a bite the first payment. Yet despite human fantasies to the contrary, a wasp, a snake, a wolf, a bird looks right through us to what we've forgotten about a bite: its transgression of meaning. A bite is nonsensical in a grammar of sin.

* * *

Belle is a biter. That's the story told about him: he takes instant dislike to most who enter, even if only with water, food, or to clean his floor. Belle has learned nothing about the benefits of playing nice. In fact, his is untainted exuberance. He rushes back and forth along the perch, or climbs the mesh screaming *Happy Birthday* then strikes a searing pose. Belle doesn't care what you say about him, to him, near him, and everyone has something to say. There is one story about Belle and he is its villain! He stares, pretty as all-get-out, poster-pretty. The punctures go very deep because Belle will not let go once he has your neck or shoulder; his talons rip clear to muscle or bone.

Tucker: *HelllNoooo!*

Sanctuary is offered, not taken.

Parrots who would never meet on any map or in any forest are bunked close with nowhere to hide, with everything hellishly visible, and everything to hide from.

At least half the macaws are skin and broken feathers—over-preened, inside-out versions of "a bird." Compulsively pruning, the smaller amazons give each other severe wounds. Over-picked cockatoos pace in bold, bald outfits of distress, or claim a tiny corner to mutilate themselves in peace. Ruin the enrichment. Destroy the trays, bowls, toys—while well-intentioned care-takers soothe and sing and attend to the lonely and deranged. A few succumb to the effort and dance.

Sometimes there's a favorite worker who relieves stress or feels just safe enough, and an intimate attachment forms. But then there's waiting in agony for the footstep, face, voice of that favorite, for every single hour they are not there. The relief of them becomes the horror of not having them. Then back to pacing or rocking. Eat your tail if you can reach it. Drill a hole straight to your heart.

"I will mutilate; I will *kill* myself!"
What creatures but those associated with humans ever do such things?

To lift a foot indicates a willingness to step up, a precious offering. A favorite worker becomes the sum of all movement, all reward, and a well-behaved bird gets carried around, at least until they try to fly, climb, jump off, or grab a bite of passing sleeve—

Adam: *Hi Adam!*

a real echo of a once-real voice,
or *vice versa*

"*Hi Adam,*" you repeat, entering the back hallway, as though everyone knows who Adam is.

You aren't Adam.

You are, however, invited to peer into Adam's reflection. It's easy to get confused in the chiaroscuro of white bodies in somber light.

Hi Adam!—three voices now.

Echo speaks the strangest banishment because hers is at once seduction, betrayal, and curse; love empty of denotation—

Zeus: *Wiggle Wiggle!*

"Adam" is she who makes the sounds *hi Adam* just as others also make "hi Adam" sounds—learned and passed around—to try the signal on—to be seen with that song, make it their own. At least five are now screaming *Hi Adam!* when you enter the cockatoo area.

Belle: *Hi Adam!*

Tucker: (*garbled radio voice*)

Adam: *Hi Adam!*

Zeus: *Wiggle Wiggle!*

* * *

Adamah: earth. Also *Adam*: one man and all mankind, and not among the animals. *Adam*, animated by breath, the sound of a vowel, made in God-likeness, the force of a word, made of no other material, the force of two words that sound alike, the way that *Adam* gets separated from *Adamah*, child-like or lacking childhood, all that one bite can pull *Adam* away from the earth, and both *Adam* and earth will suffer. The first name embodies the absence of the named thing; a form of magic.

Adam is usually first to bid for your attention: *Hi Adam!* then *Hi Adam!* twenty times more—and then her whole repertoire of tricks for claps and smiles—hanging from the wire and doing a little dance in the air with her feet, though Belle will join and do the same trick. It's impossible not to clap and respond because the performance is for you, and what kind of person doesn't acknowledge a gift? Adam pauses and looks you right in the eye when you clap; your heart sinks. An abyss. Then she starts swinging by her beak and jigging her feet again, and you realize her need is unending, and you will be the one to walk away.

Poppy: *Whatcha doin'? Whatcha doin'?*

Lucky: (*human laughter*)

Buddy: (*horse's neigh*)

Cookie: *Hello Cookie!*

Belle: *Happy Birthday!*

Rainbow: *Rainbow!*

* * *

Human touch plays dangerously with desire. The top of the head is less sensitive and the only place anyone should put their hand. Stroking a parrot's body or under their wings is a sexual come-on that leads to flooding hormones and mating arousal; a concupiscence. This only ends badly, painfully, *for there is no God before me, says the God, and I am a jealous God, there will be no one before Me.* Lust. Frustration. A joke. The bite, having occurred, cannot be undone. We accuse Adam of not "behaving herself"; of being a "bad bird"—

Rainbow lifts his foot at you. His wings are raw, his muscles unable to find flight movement, even if given the chance. A foot says "please"—encouraged, allowed—but not if he uses his beak to pull himself higher up the arm. Rainbow signals again with a foot, but when the arm comes near, he can remove a finger, tear out an eye, until shelter volunteers are driven off in need of stitches, missing ears, chunks of cheek, lip, dangerous cuts on the neck and face and arms, crying, "Why did he do that!? I was just trying to take him out!" So much wounded innocence. So many good intentions.

A bird pins you when they squint their pupil, like "Hey..." or "Oooo exciting!" Our non-verbal vocabulary is woeful, our eyes automatic.

Adam expertly mirrors your smallest offerings. It's a form of loving, isn't it, to mimic the beloved, unconsciously match vocal register, nod and agree ...

Zeus: *Wiggle! Wiggle!*

What are mirror neurons but the hardwire of seductions, of belonging—the whole way we earn our place by making ourselves fit with whomever is there. Without fitting in, no one could endure childhood, no one could survive evolution. They call it *fitness.*

Adam will live to an age that outlasts all the humans she knows: eighty to one hundred years.

She was already forty when she arrived at the sanctuary. As a baby bird, either wild-stolen, trafficked, or hand-raised, she responded to her human 'owner' as a parent, and only later, at six or seven, now adult, she falls in love and instantly becomes a refugee.

Therefore a man leaves his father and his mother and clings to his wife, and they become one flesh. What we miss when we look at the cute young bird, snuggly and peppy and friendly, is how, like most parrots, she needs to bond for life. And she'll live to love for a hundred years.

Des-pair. Pair-rot.

Lightning lifts one of her feet when the visitors pass by; just a fifty-year-old macaw waving hello, wanting your look, for you to maybe stop and wave back.

Eighty to a hundred years.

When the well-intentioned "pet owner" leaves to go shopping, or to go on vacation, to work, to grow ill, to grow old—it is merely a parting. To the parrot, it's betrayal of a soul-murdering kind. To Adam there was one rule: we are one. But too busy and overextended to think that way—our time with Adam is one obligation of many. We need to go to out, see friends, travel! We invite lovers, children, into our lives, into our beds, our house. When we're there for a few minutes, okay . . . calm . . . but for the rest of the day Adam is alone, desperate. She can't believe we don't see how lonely she feels. So she hurts herself to show us. Maybe we wake up and her stomach's plucked. Or a wing. She writes a love-letter in mutilated skin and bloody feathers.

"I'm moving"; "I'm getting married"; "I got a new job"—"What will I do with Adam?"Adam makes herself hideous.

In jungle canopy, excrement streams behind in a trail of sweetened goo not to be seen again. In a home, excrement coats the floors and furniture and needs constant cleaning. In the wild, nuts and berries get thrown around while eating so the seeds will spread. In a home, it's just more mess. Birds call so loud across thick jungle that in our house they make us deaf. They scream when we walk away, they scream when they see us. In many homes we can't abide the screaming so we lock them in small dark places, only to find they grow hysterical, scream even more, and begin to kill themselves. In the jungle there are layers of soaring melodious calls. Now in a basement, we hope no one hears as they offer desperate words all day and night. Put the bird in a drawer. Or in a garage. Cover her cage all day to force her into silence.

A betrayal exceeds all other forms of hurt, revealing that we weren't ever at home where we thought we were, and you were not who I thought you were to me, nor I to you, our bond was a lie. We didn't belong, together—here, there, or in any place. This was never a family, nothing special; its total erasure. All that echoes are meaningless sounds: "pretty bird," *phone ringing,* "I love you," *babble from the television, a dog bark,* "Polly wanna cracker?," *a catcall,* "shut up," "fuck you."

Adam: *Hi Adam!*

The message machine says the sanctuary is already full. Over 600 parrots and no money to renovate more space. They get 500–1,000 calls to take in unwanted birds every month.

No wild animal, under any circumstance, can find a home in a human place. There is no word for it. No grammar. No way to talk their way into something coherent, no matter how many phrases they learn. There remains only the bite. Then Adam is exiled when the moving van pulls away. Or stuffed in a cabinet out on a porch. Maybe with a note. Usually without water.

* * *

Disobedience seems like a *yes* or *no* answer to an easy question. Children break rules. Teenagers break rules. Middle-aged women break rules. In fact, there's likely not a living creature who hasn't disobeyed some rules. The story of God's garden follows in kind: a false conflict between freedom and survival.

The wild creature says: "Bite, you will not die."

But the God says *Yes, you will!*

Adam instantly sees that rules are mere tricks and nonsense made up by an easily frightened man. It's not eternity, but mortality, that's bliss. Fruit rots sweet and falls apart, revealing the seeds it evolved to carry; there is no death in mortality.

Springtime in captivity and one or two birds on rare occasion may bond in the sanctuary. They scrounge scraps into a makeshift nest. But there is no encouraging "brooding" because what follows would be a clutch, and that would be too devastating, even deadly. In a nest hidden well enough to evade dismantling, the eggs are removed and boiled, put back dead. There's a reason "broodiness" is selected out from domestic birds: farmers want productivity to prevail over family. Domestication eliminates claims to privacy, a life-cycle *de facto* and *de jure* already spoken for.

But captive wild animals do not accept punishment in response to bites and hiding. Those are wild ways, not wrong ones. God tries to deny Adam the wild right to deceive. Standing in naked exposure in their pens reveals our shame, not the birds'.

Very few creatures pair for life. It's hard. It's heart-breaking. Spring in captivity, there's nothing worse: chased feet, attacked hair, and every angry bite says *Why don't you love me like I love you!* Our refusal, dismissal, friendly goodbyes set off blind despair, and they are bereft, stunned, and, with nowhere to go, nowhere to belong, all is irrelevant, uninviting, excruciating. Our betrayals are more than injustice, they are the negation of life, losses that no amount of cut fruit and pasta and nuts, no scratch on the head once in a while, no perch, no plaything, no trip around the room on the food cart can undo.

So there's Adam, saying hi to herself. Doing her trick for your applause. Like most of the cockatoos, she is not in a pair-bond because she was raised by humans and has developed no affinity for birds. You intend your passing "Hi Adam" as a genuine connection. *Hi Adam!* she echoes, dancing her feet off the cage-wire.

Chief: *Hi Adam!*

George: *Hi Adam!*

George has no choice but to pace at the far end of the enclosure, in shadow. Missing the man he lived with for thirty years (who moved to a retirement village), George has eaten off his front feathers so many times they won't regrow. He wears a custom bib. You're told he likes the sunshine song, and when you sing it he dances and bobs his head, seeming less devastated for a minute.

"Hi George," you say, and he'll try to come to the wire to meet you, but Lily prevents him every time with a threatening raised crown and lunge, so he walks glumly back to the corner, though his eye stays on you, reaching out like a hand.

As you walk away from Adam and George and Lily and Chief, and take a few steps toward Zeus and Henry and Cookie, you hear *Hi Adams!* rising louder and faster—to get you to please turn and look back.

Scientists explain that how guilty we feel about what we as humans might owe other beings should depend only on a species' "encephalization quotient" (EQ). The non-linear regression formula proposes to reveal intelligence, and then equate intelligence with consciousness. A raven is 2.49, an elephant 2.36, a dog 1.2, a squirrel 1.1. Humans are 7.6.

Scientists defend their right to measure the sheer number of neurons, to sum up who is more or less conscious and intelligent. But who can make sense of neurons across species-worlds? What common problem can everyone solve? What common problem does everyone have? It turns out that the highest EQ is found in frugivores, and scientists speculate this is because locating and picking ripe fruit demands a complex, trichromatic map of visual space.

So is Adam's problem to have been born in God's garden without a flock or flight or any way to prove he can obey the right rules? "Hi, Adam!" God said in a sing-song baby-voice, wiggling his finger into the feathered belly, "Who's a Good Boy?"

Adam: *Who's a good boy?*

* * *

And the big guy said, *Let there be a living room.*
And then the guy separated the living room from the kitchen. And he saw that this was good.
So he said, *Let a garage go off the kitchen.*
And this was good, so the guy said, let's fence in some grass and add a few hydrangeas. He saw that these were good, and these are the generations of X, and the guy said, *Let us have a pet to amuse us indoors.* So he bought an illegally smuggled wild-caught pet-store parrot and named it Adam and saw that it was good. And the guy and his wife begat two children and said, *Let us talk to Adam when funny and cute, and ignore Adam when the television is on.* And the children wanted to let Adam out of the cage so the guy said, *Let the living room not be covered in shit*, and it was not so good.

And there were years and there were vacations and there were nights and days and the guy and his wife and two children saw that Adam only liked one of them now, and bit the rest if they came into the room, and screamed all the time and plucked her feathers out. Then the neighbors complained and the guy said, *Let Adam live in the basement where no one can hear.* And Adam was not in their image.

And the big guy got angry because the screams and the bloody biting were upsetting the family. Banishing the bird to the basement was not enough, so he said, *Let Adam go forth from the house, and mate-less and heartbroken will be his days.*

It seemed like that's all there was these days—the biters, screamers, liars, and those who couldn't follow simple rules—so it came upon everything that the guy said *Lo, I am going to destroy them*, said the guy, *along with the earth.*

But the guy's son Noah was a good boy, and of a kind who had learned over generations how to be docile, to listen to the guy's orders, to follow the rules, and never bite or hide, lie, steal, or fly away.

Only Noah the good boy would survive.

This time we're going to do it right, said the guy—*this time no garden, no fruit, no talking snake. This time, it's all surveillance from the get-go, all stage set and props. Flood the planet, start with that. Then we'll get a good houseboat, with cement rooms and 9-gauge steel, and good ol' Noah to steer us to Mars. No more bountiful growth, no more florid ecstasies set among unique forms of life. All will be spaceship and robots and short-snouted floppy-eared baby-faced customers. With you, my beloved pets, I shall make my zoo and covenant. You shall live in cages, two by two, under video and LED. The pairs will bond and mate in captivity, or not at all.*

Thus it was Noah that did all that. He did everything the big guy commanded, and he named and paired off pets—and lo—as the waters swelled and churned and rose up over the mountains, there was only one face upon the earth.

Zeus: *Wiggle Wiggle!*
Lily: *Hi Adam!*
Chief: (*horse's neigh*)
George: *Hi George!*

And so it was that Noah and his menagerie watched in lonely hope as the birds flew out searching for land. Coming back without any growing thing, they had nowhere to perch but on Noah's outstretched finger.

Rainbow: *Rainbow!*

HAPPY/THAT YOU HAVE THE BODY
(THE MIRROR TEST)

—

Everybody mentions the elephant in the room.

The first Chief Justice of the U.S. Supreme Court, Chief Justice Marshall, empha-sized the importance of habeas corpus, *writing in his decision in 1830, that the 'great object' of the writ of habeas corpus is 'the liberation of those who may be imprisoned without sufficient cause.'*

Habeus corpus: that you have the body
Habeus corpus relief: that you have freedom for the body

Happy lives in a solitary pen, despite the fact that elephants are herd animals and female elephants form life-long bonds. The Bronx Zoo closed its elephant program, but continues, after forty years, to hold Happy in an enclosure not larger than a few times her body length.

If the body is not a thing under common or natural law, the body may have the right not to be imprisoned, be as it may that for all beings the body itself is already a form of prison. Some prisons, for example, are very small and live fast and briefly, burdened with constant hunger or fear, while other bodies grow enmeshed with other bodies, prisons alongside prisons, layered evolution, eons of embodied wonder, color and kind morphing fortunes from below the surface to the outer atmosphere, as each prison lasts the exact length as its life, before release is secured, before forms transform, before/after the prison-body in every variety of conscious mind means everything and also nothing to other some-bodies, so that any body should imply its very release/relief to not be just a thing, ever.

The writ of habeas corpus primarily acts as a writ of inquiry, issued to test the reasons or grounds for restraint and detention.

The elephant in the room has a name, we've called her Happy. Stolen with her siblings from their herd in Thailand, named for a Disney dwarf and flown into the U.S., "that same year, Sleepy died, and the corporation relocated Happy, Grumpy, Sneezy, Doc, Dopey and Bashful to the still operational *Lion County Safari*, in Loxahatchee, Florida. Happy and Grumpy were sent to the Bronx Zoo before Grumpy was euthanized after being attacked by two other elephants. Happy is alone and has been for forty years."

NEVER FORGETS

June 15, 1215, Runnymede, near Windsor, England. King John signs the Magna Carta, of which the 29th clause says: "No man shall be arrested or imprisoned . . . except by the lawful judgment of his peers and by the law of the land."

The King, constables, even local sheriffs, had selectively locked people up, until *habeus corpus* undermined their flimsy pretexts. Centuries later, across an ocean, James Madison argued that the same protection should be written into the U.S. Bill of Rights.

MR WISE: So we must show that Happy is a person. The way we show Happy is a person is by implicating the Court of Appeals case from *Byrn* from 1972. *Byrn* made it clear that being a person and being a human being are not synonymous . . . In that case, it had to do with a person—with if it was a human being who was a fetus, the Court said that while she was still a human, a fetus was not a person. It made it clear that personhood is an issue not of biology, but it has to be a matter of public policy.

Who deserves a person's relief? Through the man-made looking-glass, creatures get tested against reflective surfaces, to see ourselves as we see them, and if they'll clean their faces as we mark them, we proclaim they've mastered our Mirror Self-Recognition test (MSR), and so possess some elusive *potential*.

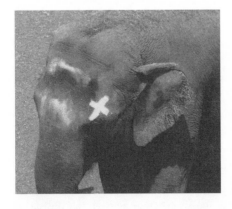

Young human children often don't want to clean their faces, and fail the test.

Happy is free-born and free-spirited, and demonstrates the definition of *free*, which is legally called "autonomy."

Autonomy asks you to decide whether or not to clean your face.

And so arguments back and forth about the nature of law, the potential elusive designation of persons, how one or the other should protect freedom and autonomy, both of which Happy could demonstrate even more if not imprisoned against her will.

THE COURT: Are you saying that maybe Happy is unhappy in the Bronx Zoo?

MR WISE: . . . Yes . . . The question is not whether the Bronx Zoo is treating her well, or whether it's not treating her well, or whether they are giving her medical care, or they are not. The question is whether or not Happy should be confined there at all.

Non-human animals mostly have one actual *right* in America—to be the recipients of trusts. So, Mr. Wise argues, let's add a second simple right: to not be arbitrarily confined. The Supreme Court already says you can't "look at a single characteristic and deprive an entity of all of the rights because of a single characteristic." Happy is an elephant. That's a single characteristic.

But the mirror splits an object from oneself, to own the potential elusive person like a piece of furniture, a king among things, to be seen and sat on, to be cared for, but also to uphold yourself and do your duty, including to be marked or ridden, if necessary, to be sold or sturdy or perhaps skinned or stuffed, if necessary, to see oneself as others do, to be humbled, in other words, as a reflection of a world that would claim to name you, to ask you to please remove that mark, to prove yourself, to make something of yourself, a mental representation, begging the question of if you have an eye, to see with it, or one to know yourself with your eyes, this external whole that sums up and idealizes what you might see of yourself, but always first a set of characteristics defined by relations and tests of tests of how one perceives oneself . . . through other eyes.

MR WISE: In 2005, Happy became the *first elephant* to pass the mirror self-recognition-test, considered to be the true indicator of an animal's self-awareness and "thought to correlate with higher form of empathy and altruistic behavior."

Staring at our reflections has also been linked to starvation and death (Narcissus).

MR WISE: One who understands the concept of dying and death must possess a sense of self. Both chimpanzees and elephants demonstrate an awareness of death by reacting to dead family or group members. Having a mental representation of the self, which is a pre-requisite for mirror-self recognition, likely confers an ability to comprehend death.

CAPTIVATING

MR MANNING/DEFENSE: One thing we do agree on is that Happy is an elephant . . . and we contend that Happy is happy where she is . . . Public policy is a legislative initiative, and not a matter for a Court . . . The Fourth Department, less than five years ago, decided another case involving a chimpanzee. Counsel referenced it as the Kiko case. I don't think the

Appellate Division misunderstood that case at all. I think they looked through the two-step transaction to find that all this is really about is changing the conditions in captivity of the elephant . . . What they are seeking to do is take Happy from an environment where she has been for forty years—

THE COURT: Forty-seven—

MR. MANNING: She has been at the Bronx Zoo for forty out of forty-seven years, Your Honor. She is comfortable there. They are trying to move Happy to some place they would rather see her . . . It's obvious that what we talked about today is the position of NHRP insofar that they seek to make persons out of animals in a variety of species, and it really has very little to do with Happy's own circumstances.

We saw our reflection imperfectly in polished obsidian, in copper, or stilled water; it got better in a metallic surface backed on glass, but sand impurities blurred us, until great sums finally gained a truer view. Now mirrors are cheap, and that non-consensual X says, "Hello crass world, you outer distortion of inner value!" The reflection asks, but does not answer, how to act when waking with this X, vestige of the master/slave dialectic on which the "mirror stage" was based: *my awareness of your awareness*, seen by Hegel as the death-struggle—one of us must prevail, and in prevailing, destroy the very awareness on which we depend. In Hegel's ritual, death is only perceived as real by the one who will become enslaved. The Master is a master because he doesn't understand his dependence on life, and therefore doesn't fear (or take into account) the reality of death—just as the Ego will go to any length to protect its premises.

(On video: two elephants walking around a small enclosure) . . .

Diana Reiss (on video): "[the Mirror Recognition Test] lets us use mirrors as a tool to see how animals process and interpret information, and it's a rare ability in the non-human animal world . . . When we first exposed a group of elephants, they explored the mirror, they actually got up over and looked over the mirror, they sniffed over the top of the wall with their trunks. One of the elephants actually tried to look under the mirror. This is similar to what we see with dolphins and great apes as well. And then once they passed this exploratory phase, they sort of check it out, similar to the Lucille Ball/ Harpo Marx skit where you sort of do a lot of repetitive movements, checking out what happens when you move a certain way . . ."

MR WISE: . . . It doesn't matter whether Happy—they think Happy is happy . . . Happy has been in prison in the Bronx Zoo for forty years. Everything about her evolution—everything about who she is as an elephant is being impinged by that every single day. She has no idea what it would be like to move to a place that's 2,300 acres where she would be able to be part of a herd and live with other elephants and make choices . . . And this is not a matter for the legislature. *Habeus corpus* in New York is a matter of common law.

(On video: dolphins in a pool moving. A chimpanzee in a tiny wire cage, poking at a screen.)

Diana Reiss (on video): "But we had to go a step further . . . the litmus test to mark an animal—we use a non-toxic child's paint—and we put a mark on one side of the elephant's head, and then an invisible mark of the same substance on the other side . . . and the idea was would they look in the mirror, see the visible mark, and touch it with their trunk, and that's exactly what this one elephant did."

(On video: Happy with white X on her face, swinging her trunk, touching the X)

STANDING/TRIAL

Maybe we succumb to the mirror as our identity takes on its spectacle—a commitment of saving face. And this we call our intelligence. Our self-awareness. That which gives us the right to call ourselves *persons*, persons with rights; image over experience. Animals, some legal experts say, can't have a person's rights—for no animal can perform the duties on the backside of the mirror: a foraging elephant tramples a farmer's property, but that elephant can't coherently stand trial, can't know right and wrong, so they say.

Mirror-mirror on the wall . . . who is the fairest of them all?

Yet doesn't the very will to autonomous life grant a right not to be deprived of it? Doesn't suffering at the hand of another confer a right to be relieved of it? Don't inflicted damages give standing, and once standing, doesn't a form of law evolve along with every animal who stands in the shadow of those laws? The experts tally those who pass through the mirror: a bottlenose dolphin, adult orangutan, adult bonobo, Eurasian magpie, pigeon, an ant, and even a cleaner wrasse fish . . .

MR WISE: The Fourth Department correctly understands that the ability of an entity to bear duties and responsibilities is irrelevant to the determination of personhood under any and all circumstances. (Mem. at Part IV.) *Graves*, 163 A.D. 3d 16; *Tommy*, 31 N.Y. 3d at 1057 (Fahey, J., concurring). An entity is a "person" if she can either bear rights or duties. *Id.* Judge Fahey made clear that it is irrelevant "that nonhuman animals cannot bear duties," as the "same is true of human infants or comatose human adults, yet no one would suppose that it is improper to seek a writ of habeas corpus on behalf of one's infant child."

How many others were marked and failed to touch the X, or joked around in the mirror because it all just seemed absurd?

HISTORY/PACING

Somerset, 1772: *Habeus corpus* success on behalf of an enslaved person. Lord Mansfield said slavery was "so odious that the common-law wouldn't support it." He said, "If you don't like what I did, then go to Parliament." They went to Parliament and they couldn't overturn it.

The U.S. Constitution mentions the term "persons" fifty-seven times, but does not define it.

Hundreds of historic cases of enslaved children given *Habeus* relief show the two-step transaction—how the first step is freedom, the second is what to do with the children, who are not "competent" to live on their own. Likewise, Happy can't go back to the wild. She is incompetent, in legal terms. After *Habeus* relief, as a world-less refugee she will need sanctuary.

MR WISE: The First Department is especially troubling by the fact they simply say, "Only humans can be persons." We say we have so been there before, because at one time, only white people could be a person. Only men could be a person. Chinese people couldn't be persons. Native Americans couldn't be persons. We have been there before. We don't need to go there again.

THE COURT: I can say this is probably the most unusual case that I've sat on in my ten years on the Supreme Court, and the twenty years prior to that working for the Court. I've always enjoyed elephants . . .

THE SINGLE CHARACTERISTIC IN THE ROOM

At night the zoo appears as a thin milky silicone holding the ghosts on a field, the stench of concrete, and dirt too hard for footprints. Feel the sensation of weakening heat, despite the infrared sensors and drones reading like text fading between lines. It's not just that fireflies have gone into childhood, that place of vivid shadows, nearly extinct, or that insects have gone into ignorance, that place burning through the retina, or that technologies that allow us to count distant stars also help us locate a few wild heat-bodies on the verge of their poaching . . . In our dying empire of predatory face data, a monkey who takes his own picture cannot own the right to his image because we look to law to diagnose selfhood, confirm our brand, crown us CEO of all species—and monkeys and elephants who may clearly express *something, only do so as human by-products, as kitsch.*

In a legal sleight of hand, even anti-cruelty laws defend the interests of "justice," not animals with rights, because animals are still personal or corporate property. Yet who is justice? How does justice have interests? Justice seems to be party to a social contract . . . and social contracts constitute citizens, not persons. Many legal attempts to protect animals rely on extending these *property* interests, in typical torts such as *malicious destruction of property.* Cruelty done to a living thing becomes therefore a sort of "property-plus"—so that cases on behalf of an animal's interest are generally denied, as the animals don't have a claim to standing on their own.

MR WISE: Excluding someone from justice, or from any social contract, doesn't mean they aren't still persons . . . as the term "person" designates the law's most fundamental category by determining who counts, who lives, who dies, who is enslaved, and who is free. *See Byrn v. New York City Health and Hospitals Corp.* (1972)

In a Florida Supreme Court case, "animal" is defined as "every living dumb creature"—reflecting how we use *speechlessness* to question the right to a day in court. How many ways are there to hear a plea?

Justice William O. Douglas, *Sierra Club v. Morton* (1972), *dissenting*: "Contemporary public concern for protecting nature's ecological equilibrium," he wrote, "should lead to the conferral of standing upon environmental objects to sue for their own preservation."

FAIREST OF THEM ALL

During the Buddha's many lives, he wasn't safe from the murderous aims of his enemies, one of whom schemed, "Verily, no mortal beholding the beauty of Gotama's person dare approach him, but the king's elephant, Najagiri, is a fierce and savage animal, and knows nothing of the virtues of the Buddha, the Law, and the Assembly."

Approaching the king's elephant-keepers, he demanded, "If you are eager for honor, early tomorrow give Najagiri sixteen pots of fiery liquor, and at the time when the ascetic Gotama comes that way, wound the elephant with spiked goads, and when in his fury he has broken down his stall, drive him in the direction of the street . . ."

(Recall the dream the Buddha's mother had at his conception: a white elephant entering her right side . . . and how later the enlightened Buddha is said to *be* a white elephant—the tamed and compassionate version of beastly *samsaric* elephants like Najagiri.)

As Najagiri charged down the street, trunk and massive legs drunken in rage, a woman dropped her child, afraid. The story tells how the Buddha stepped into Najagiri's path, and revealed to him how he'd been made drunk only to attack. Upon hearing this, Najagiri lifted the child to the side, and all the drink in his body left him.

Buddha: "Najagiri you are a brute elephant and I am the Buddha elephant. Henceforth be not fierce and savage, nor a slayer of men, but cultivate thoughts of charity." And he taught him the Law.

BLIND EXPERT FEELS THE TAIL

"Any case that could lead to billions of animals having the potential to file lawsuits is a shocker in the biggest way" (Richard Cupp, Pepperdine Law School). "Once you say a horse or dog or cat can personally sue over being abused, it's not too big a jump to say, 'Well, we're kind of establishing that they're legal persons with that. And legal persons can't be eaten.'"

Animal birth, the Buddha taught, is the worst birth—most unfortunate and without hope. Supposedly lacking any means to understand their circum-stances, animals die in terror and pain, with no intelligence through which to make spiritual progress. A blind turtle never actually sticks its head through that floating ring. "The bondage of the animal realm" means dwelling in disease-ridden muck, eating shit, being born and dying in water, being born and dying in darkness, rot, eating infested and decomposing flesh, and suffering the most repulsive and tortured lives imaginable. Not only that, animals are said to live by "the law of the fish" where justice only means bigger eats smaller, on and on without end. Worst of all, the Buddha taught, no one in the animal realm can reach enlightenment—can ever attain the "fruit of stream-entry."

Buddha is reborn as an elephant seven times, for nothing is as dangerous as taming a wild mind. But in reality, there was no meditative magic: the malicious and violent beatings by the *mahout* rendered elephants submissive, just as the bullwhips, electric prods, and solitary confinement of modern zoo-keepers exact the cruel obedience.

Still, by ostensibly *taming* Najagiri, it was said that the Buddha caused entire crowds to attain enlightenment. It was nothing less than an old-fashioned miracle, a perfect advertisement. Waste your precious human life, the Buddha taught, and the billions of ways you can blow it are the billions of unfortunate hell-bound animals born every day.

IF YOU'RE HAPPY AND YOU KNOW IT

State v. Fessenden (2014): "As we continue to learn more about the interrelated nature of all life, the day may come when humans perceive less separation between themselves and other living beings than the law now reflects. However, we do not need a mirror to the past or a telescope to the future to recognize that the legal status of animals has changed and is changing still[.]"

When Buddha was enlightened for just ten short years, he went alone to the forest of Pārileyyaka to recover from feuding among his monks. In this forest, an elephant who had lost his herd served the Buddha "as a mirror"—sensing and fulfilling his every need and wish. The elephant would move enormous rocks into the sun and then into the pool to heat the bath water. The elephant would fan the man, and feed him, and keep the sleeping area clear. At night the elephant would stalk the forest with a large club to protect him. Together the elephant and the Elephant-Among-Men spent the rainy season, until they both felt refreshed.

Brussels, France, New Zealand, Quebec, Switzerland, Slovakia, Austria, and Egypt have all redefined animals as *sentient beings* and not things or property. As the *Slovak Spectator* reports: "animals will enjoy special status and value as living creatures that are able to perceive the world with their own senses. Provisions on movable things apply to animals, but not if it contradicts the nature of an animal as a living creature."

A writ was issued on behalf of an orangutan named Sandra in Buenos Aires, Argentina, in 2015. One year later, another Argentine court recognized a chimpanzee named Cecilia as a "non-human person," ordered her released from a Mendoza Zoo pursuant to a writ of *habeas corpus*, and sent her to a sanctuary.

In *United States ex rel. Standing Bear v. Crook* (C.C. Neb. 1879), the court rejected the United States Attorney's argument that no Native American could ever be a "person" able to obtain a writ of *habeas corpus*, and issued a writ on behalf of the Ponca chief, Standing Bear.

The Indian Supreme Court held that nonhuman animals have both a statutory and a constitutional right to personhood and certain legal rights. *Animal Welfare Board v. Nagaraja* (2014).

On March 20, 2017, New Zealand declared the Whanganui River a legal person after its headwaters were diverted, its bed was mined and straightened, its rocky falls flattened, its fish populations killed, and the water polluted. Now a forest and a mountain will become legal people, too.

In 2018, the Colombian Supreme Court designated its part of the Amazon rainforest as "an entity subject of rights," in other words, a "person."

In April 2020, the Chief Justice of the Islamabad High Court determined that animals have natural and legal rights, and ordered a solitary elephant, Kaavan, freed from the Marghazar Zoo. In contemplating the pandemic in which we find ourselves, he writes: "Has nature forced the human race to go into 'captivity' so as to make it realize its dependence for survival on other beings possessed with a similar gift, i.e., life?"

MR WISE: This case will turn on whether an extraordinarily cognitively complex and autonomous nonhuman being such as Happy should be recognized as a legal person with the right to bodily liberty protected by the common law of *habeas corpus* pursuant to a New York common law that keeps abreast of evolving standards of justice, morality, experience, and scientific discovery, and an evolving New York public policy which already recognizes certain nonhuman animals as "persons" (Mem. at Part I). As recently recognized by Court of Appeals Associate Justice Eugene Fahey in *Tommy*, this question is "a deep dilemma of ethics and policy that demands our attention." Further, "[t]he evolving nature of life makes clear that chimpanzees and humans exist on a continuum of living beings . . . To solve this dilemma, we have to recognize its complexity and confront it."

From the *Mahavibhasa*: *At the beginning of an eon, during an eon of evolution, all beings use the Saintly language (i.e. Sanskrit). But later, when they eat and drink, the division between beings becomes unequal; insincerity and hypocrisy grow; also, there are all sorts of languages, and a point is reached where there are some beings who are no longer capable of speaking.*

A few months ago, an elephant in a South African game park killed a poacher hunting for black rhinos. The elephant took the poacher's body to a place where it could be eaten by lions.

After his refreshing sojourn in the forest, when the Buddha was ready to return to the town, he told the loyal elephant that despite their bond, the elephant had to stay behind: "Pārileyyaka, I am not turning back! In your present state of existence, you cannot attain the transic states, nor insight, nor the fruits of the path. You must stay here!"

At hearing these words, the elephant tucked his trunk and retreated. Dying of a broken heart, he hoped that something would change the Enlightened One's mind.

The elephant in the room can do nothing but wait.

TURNS BEFORE THE CURTAIN

—

TUMBLEWEED

An innocuous bramble cavorts onstage.

Plague! Disaster! Rampage!
"Biological pollution can't be reversed!"

The audience giggles at the silly rolling—

Surprise! Ten thousand interlocking tumbleweeds bounce aggressively up into the grid, up and beyond the set, up the aisles, choking the exits—it's high noon in the old west!

No more giggles.

Tumbleweeds came from "Eurasia."

Where is that? Why did they send these marauding carcasses here?

Clowns enter—a high-kicking number—sending more tumbleweeds onto the audience.

Clowns!

Sunlight stretches across the drought-parched range where ranchers can't support their herds. No cattle eat the strange young plants who have ample room to spread out in the denuded soil. Why does no one eat these shoots?

A sudden rain and the happy plants reach their potential, tall as you please.

Come winter, the tall green dies back to brown. Frost and wind uproot the twisted spools who perambulate far and wide, clumping and romping and intertwining, blocking schools and roads and fences. Tumbleweeds seek adventure across all habitable and uninhabitable space. The windy season is for breaking loose and setting sail, for spreading more seed than can ever be counted! Ah, destiny.

MAPS

So where is "Europe?" If you ask a fungus, maybe it starts in Moscow and travels westward at 41 kilometers a year. Maybe it reaches Sweden from its Asiatic origins.

Confused clapping. Who cares where Europe is? It's everywhere and nowhere, so what?

But the fungus didn't start in Moscow. It started in "Asia." Where is Asia?

It is a continent of itself, but only by convention. Is a continent more or less a discrete landmass surrounded by water? What's a large island? Where is Asia and where is Europe? Is there a reason to cross from one to the other?

Often, it's left to the Isthmus. Does this audience even think about Africa?

The first chemical reaction, the know-how of fire, spread among early humans just as human populations spread out of Africa—north and east and west, bringing combustion for cooking, space-travel, and cars that pass tiny particles along arteries.

Someone yells *Fungi*! in the crowded theater.

Fomites everywhere: an accumulation of home, nation, fashion, and custom (from Latin *fomes*—the word for tinder, the ignition for the contagion)—

Exiting things leave carbon scattered on stage: bones, wood, coal, lava . . . Plants tangle their breath, absorb radioactive carbon dioxide from the universe. Lumbering animals acquire it from eating the plants.

Fat men in hats point to a star chart of possible earths.

Languages die.

Fungi gain their own "kingdom," like a bright royal place apart from plants and animals where "growth is their main means of mobility, except for spores, which may travel through air or water . . . " Mostly they live in soil, or on things already dead.

FERAL SWINE

Raucous horn section. Stampedes. Police at the exits. Everyone carries poison. After releasing pigs in new-world forests, Europeans bring in wild boar to shoot as well.

"Everyone is affected in some way!"
"We can't just barbeque our way out!"

Feral piglets run down the aisles with youthful acrobatics. Their lack of natural predators makes them giddy! They are hybrids of hybrids, but if not all non-natives are invasive, and not all invaders are non-native, what, for example, do we do with the *bristly pig*, descendant of escaped farm animals?

Don't be fooled! These cuties grow to 5 feet long and 3 feet high and weigh up to 250 lbs! Running up to 30 mph, they have cloven devil hooves and skin that can withstand assault rifles shot from low-flying helicopters! Worse, they breed year-round—doubling their population in only 4 months.

A feral pig dies agonizingly slowly from a gunshot, while others, wallowing, pollute springs and ponds and alter stream beds and habitat because no one wallows who doesn't also root.

Put more bounty on feral hogs, it doesn't stop their families spreading like wildfire across state lines, carrying disease, damaging crops, eating endangered species—not to mention whole pig clans tearing up archeological sites!

Archeological sites?

Denmark builds a 70 km fence along its border with Germany. Will the pigs stop crossing? Will African swine fever, which has been found in two dead boar in Belgium, threaten Denmark's huge pig industry? Feral removal programs include aerial hunting, surveillance, and cage and corral traps.

In America, the feral pig population grows from 1 million to over 6 million across 38 states.

A pig runs past the curtain, escapee from a farm; another tiptoes in from a hunting preserve. They feed on endangered birds' eggs, young lambs, crops, snakes, and ladies' hats. Always on the move, they split up to protect their babies, jumping fences, swimming across lakes, cutting through fields, hiding along riverbanks, diverting attention to escape the dogs and night hunts—

The government enters with a plan: Warfarin (sold as *Kaput Feral Hog Bait*) will poison them, and, bonus, turn their insides blue to warn hunters not to cook them for dinner.

"If you want them gone, this will get them gone."

In a part of Australia, Warfarin eliminates 99% of feral pigs in a few months. But immobilized pigs, bleeding from their eyes and dying for weeks in helpless pain, bring too much outcry, and the poison is phased out in favor of the low-flying helicopters and assault rifles.

Long shrill noise, microphone feedback—no, it's a garbled announcement:

The UN Working Group on Invasive Alien Species: *wah wah, wah WAH, wah wah wah*

Laughter. What's so funny?

Humans have lived in Florida for 12,000 years. Ponce de Leon arrived in 1513 and began recording "history." Florida has historic and prehistoric sites within 8 inches of the surface being rooted up and ruined by wallowing feral swine.

Feral swine for an encore!

Making silly faces they root around everyone's business, toss ancient artifacts, splatter mud on the front row, eat everyone's gummy bears.

Arrest them!

UN Representative: *The introduction of invasive alien species as pets, aquarium and terrarium species, and as live bait and live food is a subcategory of "escape" as a pathway. Escape is the pathway of organisms from captivity or confined conditions into the natural environment. Through this pathway the organisms are initially intentionally imported or transported into the confined conditions, then escape.*

RABBITS

All 305 global rabbit species descend from maternal lines of two isolated herds 12,000 years ago, one in Spain and one in southern France.

Greek and Roman conquerors, not knowing what to call these odd, quiet animals, dubbed the region "Rabbit-Ridden." Meanwhile, no original or single word exists in English: Cony" "Rabbidge" "Rabbert" "Rabbet" "Rabatte" "Rabytt"—

So cute!

Finland, empty of rabbits.

Europeans rush on and dump bunnies on Finland.

They dump more on Tasmania, Australia, and before anyone can look away, the entire stage is rabbits—devouring violets and chrysanthemums off the graves in the Helsinki cemetery. With their tiny mouths and picky eating, they eat seedlings before they reproduce. This eliminates new growth of the ancient steppe, and makes other mammals, reptiles, and birds starve.

Not so cute!

Rabbits dig under nets that would have stopped a wild hare. Rabbits scurry and climb and are weirdly good at getting around obstacles and aren't particularly afraid of anything. They reject the wooded areas and invade the parks and burrow under the paths and beds.

Scientists trod around, pointing out rabbit warrens marked with dunghills.

No one can clear rabbits offstage.

By law, you can only kill rabbits in Finland with bow and arrow.

This is intolerable!

Citizens of Helsinki take the law into their hands. Rabbits are shot anywhere they appear, stabbed by hayforks, dungforks, trapped, hit by special pneumatic air-guns, or set on by cats. None of it is legal, but people openly reject the law and the official "hunting season." Patrol platoons of stagehands set poison and carry rifles out in the city parks and along the back streets, while the Head Gardener, Pesu, kills a hundred a day with his rifle. He waves a special permit.

Uruguay, 1930—a lab full of rabbits. Scientists run onstage spreading the myxoma virus.

Tumors grow and bacterial infections kick in. All the lab rabbits die.
The virus enters Australia and most rabbits fall dead—from 60 to 100 million!
A few remaining bunnies develop immunity.

A farmer rushes into France with the virus.

By 1954, 50% of feral and wild rabbits are gone. The skin of a diseased rabbit
is sent from London to Ireland so Irish farmers can rub it on healthy rabbits
who are then driven by car and released around the country.

Resistance to the virus spreads.

Scientists make a new RHD2 virus that enters the rabbit population.

They sicken. Many who would hide emerge and are shot.

The Gardener stands center stage. The rabbit menace has been stopped in
Helsinki because of the new virus brought from Europe; the second strain.

Dance number.

The virus carries by respiration, hairs, anything the rabbit touches or breathes
on, even on the wind. Infected rabbits stay contagious for 2–200 days. The
virus only kills rabbits, but fleas, flies, foxes, anyone else can give the virus
back to rabbits. Infection kills within a few days, with fever, squealing, convul-
sions, and coma leading to last little breaths. Most rabbits die in the privacy
of their underground burrows.

**Cameras capture these deaths and project them on screen, so everyone
can be absolutely sure.**

Younger rabbits are immune due to their immature systems. They sit aban-
doned and terrified.

Rabbits run in a dotted line as far north as Tuusula on the map.

In their native habitat in Spain, Portugal, and southwestern France, the European rabbit is practically extinct due to a highly infectious Lago-virus that spread westward from China, where it decimated the Chinese population of European angora rabbits.

Scientists take that virus over to Australia to control those rabbits.

The virus escapes the quarantine in 1995, and kills 10 million rabbits in 8 weeks.

New Zealand farmers put dead rabbits in kitchen blenders to spread the virus after the government decides not to introduce it to the island. But the farmers didn't get the memo that rabbits under 8 weeks old are immune, and they release the virus just after breeding season so all the babies survive. Not only that, but resistance to the disease among rabbits in New Zealand requires the use of aerial spreading of poison as well.

A few Korean scientists release a new strain of the virus they believe kills rabbits better in wetter conditions.

Vaccines against both the myxoma and the RHDH viruses are available through much of the world to protect pet rabbits, except in Australia where policy-makers fear the resistant rabbits will escape and join the feral population.

BOATS

Fanning their faces, the audience follows the cargo being unloaded and loaded and traded and moved along the dotted routes from all continents and countries, docking in every port—

Why do boats get their own laws, and can just go anywhere they want?

The dock-workers and shipmen sing *We Are the World, we are the children* . . .

Seriously, who needs so many air conditioners?

A generation of accidental fugitives flies and crawls and swims and seeds and spreads from the tankers and containers, each more talented than the last, each with a few tricks more effective, each hair-raising turn more daring and enthusiastic, passing it all to their excited offspring, happy children without predators, without disease, without competition . . .

What lovely ornamental plants! What pest-free varieties! What exotic pets! What delicious delicacies!

The loudspeaker crackles with a recording of the *Nonindigenous Aquatic Nuisance Prevention and Control Act* WAH WAH WAH-WAH

OMG! Turn that off! That hurts our ears!

Lines of yellow-bodied Mediterranean oleander aphids, glimmering emerald ash borers, and jaunty house sparrows take positions on every available arm-rest, preening and snacking and egg-laying.

Iridescent starlings display balletic swoops. They roost in the lights and forage every inch of stage, where Kousa dogwood, multiflora rose, kudzu, and alder buckthorns have darkened the floor. The lights no longer penetrate the somber scene, and under the weight of the vines the scenery collapses.

Norway maples, Asian hornets, snakeheads, and Asian longhorn beetles show off synchronized kicks and twirls in every last remaining inch—*one two three kick!*—celebrating this new-found paradise!

On and on the performers grow annoying. Then onerous. Then downright offensive!

Where is the rest of the program? Is the backstage empty? Are the dressing rooms empty? Isn't anyone waiting in the wings? Where are the stage managers and staff?

The emcee is asleep in the piano-player's lap. The boats have long since sailed.

(faint echo) We are the world . . .

This'll bore us out of house and home!

The houselights flicker with a million mouth-parts smacking, twigs breaking, and larvae crawling—all in a cheerfully monotonous chorus turned deafening.

O Captain! my Captain!

The piano-player elbows the emcee, who presses play on a recording of the *Alien Species Prevention Enforcement Act WAH wah WAH wah*

The available oxygen is being used up!

Wah WAH wah WAH WAH wild mammals, wild birds, fish, mollusks, crustaceans, amphibians, and reptiles are the only organisms that can be added to the injurious wildlife list wah wah wah

Injurious Wildlife? Roundup them up! Give 'em the hook!

Little elbows lock in triumph—a billion beautiful, talented, daring, prodigious performers, from every end of the world—

.

"We slayed!"
"We killed!"
"We knocked 'em dead!"

What impossible acts to follow!

PLASTIC

Except a furtive cohort of little nurdles on the move.

Nurdles slip and slide through tiny crevices and cracks, pearly as monarch eggs, they don't become larvae, and glisten instead forever at the tide-line, in the space between seats, in the petals of grass, bopping down tiny creeks, joining waterways and beaches into a stained petro-chemical blur.

Nurdles?

A hose nozzle. Some sacks leak. Pipes seep. Nurdles spill from so many joints. Not-alive but—

Look! The boats are back! There's barely room at the ports!

Nurdle powder rises up the nose. Nurdles rise into shirt cuffs, down the socks, up the panties, deep as snow, light as a breeze.

What the hell is this stuff?

Diagrams of science-y things: Broken bedrock. Shale deposits. Land and sea empires of petro-chemical companies. A nuisance byproduct molecule of fracking that made it near unprofitable.

Little Ethane enters. So cute!

Big Men jog onstage, tossing out goody-bags of flimsy toys, socks, t-shirts, and little cell phones.

PR guy: It took millions of years to make that molecule!

They grab Ethane by the collar, lift him in their arms.

PR guy: But in one tremendous heating process, we can crack the shit out of that shit, and make it *ethylene*! And you know what ethylene becomes . . .

The Big Men lift little Ethane onto their shoulders—

"Our Hero!" they lead everyone in clapping and smiles.

Nurdles bob in the water at the high-tide, cling to the sandy shore or wedge themselves into the smallest pebbles and stone.

Nurdles are cheap. Nurdles are slippery. Dented nurdles pick up contaminants and carcinogens. Floods of cheap nurdles have nowhere to go. Nurdles wake up on the beaches in high numbers, looking just like fish and horseshoe crab eggs. Puffins in Scotland and shearwaters in Australia have nurdles in their stomachs.

It's a renaissance! Virgin plastic is cheaper than recycled plastic for the very first time ever!

New ethane plants dot the Gulf Coast, financed by Saudi companies, and along Louisiana waterways by South African companies. Ports like Houston run out of space for tankers loading up nurdles for Asia and Europe.

50% of the world's plastics are younger than 15 years old! Adolescents: fast, cheap, and out of control!

But a few dedicated nurdle-hunters creep around the beaches collecting "evidence." They go to Scotland and Belgium, where new petrochemical hubs are sprouting up. Even a few single-use-plastic bans would slow the profits, and already thirty-four African countries are saying, "No thank you, single-use plastic!" Even China! France! The boats look a little glum.

What? Where will all the poor American nurdles go?

The Big Men twist their moustaches and laugh! Governments will bail us out. They'll ban the plastic bans! There are no laws against nurdles! They haven't been regulated anywhere, and most people don't even know they exist!

Nurdles go wherever the currents take them. Older nurdles turn yellow and brown, like fossil teeth floating around the oceans.

TRUE CRIME/NATURE FAKERS

—

Consider if [definition: house] is not the same as [5 synonyms for house] or any of [6 words used for the living spaces of animals].

Recall [3 things we see when a hand draws a frame], and then [10 things outside the frame]—especially if there is a [definition: animal] in it, or outside it.

Consider [4 signs of drought], [3 forms of environmental degradation], and [10 recent large-scale disasters]

Consider [3 kinds of animals that break into houses]

Consider [definition: "criminal"]

i.e., "a fox came in, house-wise, and became me and was no longer wild because it was housed through me, *as me* almost, as if in a primal crime-scene. The fox did things in my place, and stood for me in ways I can and can't stand, and its eyes flickered with particularity, as though this one fox was now a family member who would know my food and arrange my clothes and pillows, just like someone I know, or who would know me, name-ish-ly. This fox in my chair left me presents like a lover or child would, cursed me, undermined me, and stole precious items like a lover or a child would. In this particular fox I saw what I see only when it looks through my things, through my self-organized rooms."

[4 differences between a mirror and a house]

[2 times someone told you to "be reasonable"]

cf. "You have the look of the beast!"

Step to the front stoop, make the call to the police. Help! (you might say). [2 descriptions of physical violence] and [1 definition: "sin"]

[3 differences between a wolf and a dog]

[definition: "prison"]

i.e., "in my house, [5 bad habits] or [2 bad intentions] aren't enough to dehumanize me. Evil is the skin-thing, the arrangement of puzzle-parts (ears, hair, muzzle, paws)—things I blame for any bodily break-in when hitting my child or peeing in the yard; the beast takes the blame."

[5 sentence recap of literary naturalism]

[definition: "instinct"]

i.e., "Who would believe another burglary? Of course it's a she-wolf, sniffing my blood, my ovum, the coil of my loins, sharing this space, yeasty wine in barrels. Trying to cross the hall, she licks my bowls and unshelves my ceramics, a lamp, paws at the sheets until a noise becomes her noise in my throat, all because [2 ways to break a rule] or [3 stories of trespassing] don't capture the feeling of being captured. The encroacher?"

[definition: "myself"]

[definition: "fairy tale"]

[definition: "convict"]

cf. "Is this not my street? Forest? My field? My driveway? Is this not my hide out? Is this not my timber frame? My toilet? My [self-serving phrase]? Did that wolf not wear my skimpiest nightie and flounce in it?"

[definition: "privilege"]

[2 ways to know if it's a lone wolf or part of a pack]

[definition: "private property"]

[3 ways to leverage the pack against a wolf]

[definition: "unconscious bias"]

O lectori salutem!

i.e., "In my house, [4 forms of violence] don't make me beastly. I'm master because my house is home to [3 'real' characters], squirrel-faced, rat-faced, pig-faced children, and we fight over food and something else, sex maybe. We leave the door open and some bears break the door anyway, break the frame right off and then argue about bowl-sizes and beds. What is it with some bears!? Then they blow the house down and leave with it. Theirs is weather all over the floor. Theirs is garbage that legislates. The frame inside their noses, scat, fur smelling up their caves."

[definition: "felonious"]

[definition: "rumor"]

If it's not part of a [definition: "metaphor"] get the [definition: "animal"] out, the neighbors say. We can't legislate this shit. [3 maladaptive behaviors] go only so far before the police show up, trailed by reporters, forensics, spectators. Do they not know [3 differences between "history" and "natural history"] or are they just going to repeat [3 animal romance tales]?

Instead: yelling at the officers, "Why don't you investigate 'alphabet,' 'animals,' 'animated,' the 'animus,' 'beast within', and please don't stop till you get all the way to 'zoo!'"

[definition: "kinship"]

[4 differences between a chimpanzee and a human]

[5 social skills]

[definition: "ego"]

Oh, puhleeze. The first detective steps toward us, warily giving a quick [definition: "due process"] and leans to his partner for [4 examples of surveillance technology], then all about how, from previously [definition: "wild"] places, they've got some fuzzy images up online, mug shots, wolves, they think, if we'd take a look. "We will definitely get them if they're still in the [definition: "neighborhood"]" and even if they're not, they're dead meat. The sound of cocking. The knowing smile.

[definition: "cage"]

[definition: "natural rights"]

i.e., Possessed by possessions, [definition: "self-haunted"] and [3 things that are hunted] until the media stops garnishing [3 recent news items about animals] for the sake of [definition: "person"].

Advertisement: the law brings you good fences and depositions, in real time, or, if we must be historical about it, [definition: "precedent"], a 17th century rooster laid an egg and got burnt at the stake, and a pig was hung high for killing a baby. Who is and isn't a [definition: "member"] of society?

Even under social pressure, our bleached-out [definition: "imagination"] does not break or bend, as if it were made of [6 eternal ideas] or [5 indestructible materials].

[definition: "witness"]

Ask the officer on call if he heard someone say witness or "whiteness"?

A witness: "I swear there wasn't anyone else home. I don't know how the animals could have got inside except by magic, or demonic trickery."

A thought bubble: possession is most of the law (of nature, too, ma'am—an uncomfortable laugh, so obvious). A crowded thought: Who has keys to the same house?

Who wrote the "yellow journalism of the woods"? Who dared transpose [1 human activity] into [3 qualities of your favorite woodland creature] without morals, without ethics, without admitting how the stories were [definition: "unrealistic"] or chock full o' [2 kinds of analogy]. It's as though [5 forms of *reportage*] must already be false, whether on a [definition: "blank page"] or [3 forms of broadcast media], or on a pre-historic wall, lit by pre-historic flames. If [1 wild animal] leads to expert testimony, then knowing [how to pay attention] or [how to see if someone is hungry, thirsty or bored] could let evidence slip away.

The detective flips open his notebook and reads off [4 creatures impossible to catch on camera], saying, "Soon, 'live' is not going to happen. It's not what people are going for."

i.e., "[any animal] would be less elusive than [2 online testimonies] or [a self-negating idea], not to mention [3 ways to manipulate video footage]— and the slightest breeze that moves a hair on your head, or dusts off your credenza, will indicate they've stolen the scene."

ipso facto, a pettifogger offers opinions, says, "The very [definition: "point of view"] lets me consider [3 examples of animal amorality] and [5 bad choices]. I won't neglect to mention, along with [4 common excuses for being less than perfect], that the [1 wild animal] was always already the bad-guy."

"Is it possible that they still thought they lived here?"

i.e., "a home of relationships and not structures?"

If you consider [3 differences between relationships and structures] and if you consider your small life on the one hand, and then compare the house-wares, the lease, the neighbor coughing up an alibi, and finally [what it means to set a thief to catch a thief], then maybe [3 differences between the documentary and the subject of the documentary] implicate the framer instead of the builder, or the designer instead of the object, the landlord instead of . . .

The officers of the law look hungry, their tongues a bit out, poking at their phones.

That's a lot of [definition: "mud"] to sift through, *eo ipso* they seem to be drifting into the house, invoking danger, or causing it.

"They went that way!" the detectives deflect—over the meadow and off the path, the boots that storm the stream, kicking it out of its banks, and hands that swirl into the pools, scaring up fish. From the air, there are drones to help shoot any escapee.

[3 examples of remote or inaccessible wilderness]

[2 imaginary creatures]

The police want to make tracks, or at least they're jumpy, the understory beckoning, or threatening, with cameramen, reporters, dogs, horses, guides and followers, the president or mayor: they enter, exit, penetrate, cross lines, and circle. Some coffee, then the search party.

[3 kinds of evidence inadmissible in court]

"We could draw out [1 wild animal] into [1 moral virtue] and we'd get [6 things fear will make someone do]. Whose fault is [4 animal-images from recent news]? How will we ultimately decide [the difference between an image and a zoo] if all that we have are [4 beast fables] and [10 animals near extinction] to go on? In other words, there's no way you couldn't have done it, or that you're free to go."

Are you calling me a "nature faker" or a bleeping animal lover? Am I built of straw or sticks, some naive activist, that some Roosevelt should doubt my tale?

i.e. "[2 animals that get trapped in wire fences] blow the alibis of [4 famous criminals]—and what with shopping, babies crying, or the time it takes to dig up dinner—maybe I was drunk or raving mad? Maybe birds broke the glass, or that cougar licked my hair?"

The night shadow and the lit windows beckoned?

[2 types of insects] entered in swarms of twos and threes, tied me up in knots?

Give me [3 examples of the "law of large numbers"] and I'll show you [4 endangered mammals] demanding "raw meat," a night foray of fighting, bones excessively chewed—and in the morning, caught on camera, it's all survival of the protagonist—

President Roosevelt (interrupting): "The very sublimity of absurdity!"

cf. That bulldog didn't kill that wolf, Mr. Jack London, the President says so.

The President says he knows about who is strong and who is a poser. *Domestic* is both the condition of the house, and the condition of the feral, but it's never going to get me/anyone off the hook for weird racism and dog stories.

[3 examples of "the law of love," "the law of evolution," or "the law of nature"]

Mr. London, taking the stand, holds up the hand-mirror to his [definition: "savages"] and his (less-evolved) monkeys, to prove that "definitions must agree not with egos, but with life."

[definition: "lone wolf"]

[definition: "feral dog"]

Mr. London, raising his hand: "Definitions cannot rule life. Definitions cannot be made to rule life. Life must rule definitions or else the definitions perish."

[4 fictional animals]

Next witness: "He was clearly mixing imagination with the truth."

Reporter: "People are saying he's the worst of the nature-faker offenders."

cf. "That lynx never could match [the dog] one on one, Mr. London."

Who says?

"The President." (And other "knowledgeable men of the hunt.")

Getting riled, you can't frame that poor animal with your crime—

i.e., Hobbes: *Isn't all man a wolf to the other man?*

cf. *Wayeeses*, I was ready to take you in and give you a medal of honor, you old white wolf, you fictional romantic figure—

("I know that as President I ought not to do this—")

i.e., "It's impossible for you to both escape and behave, because, due to counter-claims, these are my things, those are my books you're drooling on, that's my mirror you're licking."

Good news! "We found a few individuals we can bring in for testing." Drugged and dragged, maybe one died, we snapped them in pictures, no context, but mugs, you know . . . what happened out there? Rewind, we hear "the hunter caused the naturalist to do strange things . . ."

Witness: *La bête sais pourquoi elle est bête.*

The judge bangs on things, but the perp's not giving anything up. Bailiff banging. More shuffling. This courtroom's bust. Make them speak! screams the character witness, as the paper flutters over deaf ears, the bantam, the hullabaloo, the irrationality of so many.

Returning from the lab, all under control, bagged and tagged, samples deposed, pinned and flayed, sliced, my sample tissues, the scientist won't even feel welcome in this white space, this [definition: "purity"].

I call the Faithful Stranger. Expert bystander. *Amicus curiae.*

Report: The search team closed the hidey-holes. They filled in the caves so no cub or kit could nap by accident. There isn't room for innocence *in camera* when [10 "dangerous" archetypes] lurk.

Be like [definition: "shame"] and get yourself buried.

The detectives boil when they're finally on the stand; eyes blank as dinner plates before dinner.

testimony: *e pluribus unum* and [definition: "5W's and How"]

The prosecutor replays the desperate fox steaming up the nanny-cam, opening the chips, stepping out for a smoke.

"Call in the accused. Tell her we know everything."

I'm counting to ten—then thinking of turning myself in—*ex malo bonum!*

(a bit of the hair of the dog, a reporter mutters.)

e.g., [3 effects of homelessness]

Yes, well, *ex post facto* to you, says the defense, and was anyone *actually* hurt? Are there any seeing *eye*-witnesses? Please take your politicians out of my twisted box of problem statements. They've appeared in the hallway, rebutted the china. When you've done something for the right whales, then we'll talk.

The politicians stand around some gadgets, reading about themselves. The jury is selected but isn't here.

e.g., "A body was eaten and [3 kinds of remains] remain."

The remains have waivers and warrants and writs, the whole clemency turned inside-out, a window-frame open and condemned, inking the night of predators in uniform, virus by morning, compensatory hunger (the one that should do all the eating), and them that makes the footprints—

[definition: "the elements of circumstance"]

verbatim, a bad detective, rotates a version of [definitian: "crying wolf"], and, needing to get someone arrested, yells, "Before they come get you, before the so-called wild disappears, I'm gonna be forced to kill it—*veni, vidi, vici*"—

[definition: "plea"]

[definition: "auto-immune"]

[3 kinds of bail]

Quick! Find someone who isn't *an officer, make a complaint where the home* is an eminent domain; *extra-territorial.*

[2 differences between guilt and personification]

[3 meanings of "parole"]

It's house arrest and we should be there. Being human, I continue to blame the beast in me.

[definition: "hearing"]

[definition: "probation"]

i.e., "Finally: a sigh. a smile. a look of fear and recognition."

[3 animal heroes and what they did]

[4 types of "figurative language"]

cf. "Why is everything in a book always about something else?"

[2 ways to close an argument]

UNSEEN

—

1.

what is unseen becomes believed
—a hell we act on—
becomes the next thought, a birth,
a spell cast with snake-strike force;
expressing, then swallowing
shadows

here: senseless human fences
tear a pregnant wolf limb from limb
and build a shaky barrier which starts on earth
and disappears

2. The *demon* is

—that which is cast—
can't find peace, place
right-spirit turned nasty
haunting commuters with unskilled noise
nonsense shreds of gutted rage
hurled at anyone (turn and yell, curse them, anything)
to steal even hate-filled words for a name

and naming themselves in the noise of strangers,
find a way to stay.

3. grave

utburd utterly lost,
tongue-dangerous,
sum of a shadow of a baby exposed
starved between roots and trees in a coffin hole
a few hours old and nobody's claim
deformed or not, drooling
oily leaves glimmer, plastic, eternal
fungus and mold, *here here*
uttering broken grammar
placenta dried in dirt
devoid, this spore of ghost
jumps your back
the forest weighing you
down on night roads
seed your hollow head
sink your spine, *there there*
with every shrieking sound on earth
every murmur, consoling, I have no throat:
  stocking, ribbon, kerchief, lace
  all tied in the throat's place
a howling weightless soundless
name upon me, throw any, please
"Shut up, Blabber-mouth" "What do you want, bratty child!"
[1 noun] [1 proper noun] [1 animal]
So here's the sum, some labels at last
[1 insult] [1 tender lullaby] [1 disease]
Murder *utburd* *gast* named (rest)

4. How to Render Oneself Invisible

A small orange image of wax in the shape of a man
in the month of January and the hour of Saturn

and write with a needle above the brow
upon its skull which thou shall have adroitly raised:

[1 wish]

After which thou shalt replace the skull in proper position
and write upon the strip of the skin of a frog
which thou shalt (not) have killed:

[something "unreal"]

And thou shalt then go and suspend the figure
by one of the hairs of your head
from the vault of a cavern at the hour of midnight
perfuming it properly and say:

Mach, Venibbeth, Beroth, Melekh, Metatron, and all ye, I conjure
thee
O Figure of Wax, that by the virtue of these Characters and
Words
Thou render me invisible wherever I may be

and bury it in a small deal box
at the place where two roads cross.

LIBERTY/TREES

—

"The distinction between freedom and liberty is not accurately known;
naturalists have never been able to find a living specimen of either."
Ambrose Bierce

Resistance

Scientists surround a yellow poplar in Annapolis
        alive more than 400 years
        and last surviving of 13 original Liberty Trees
  "in pretty poor shape" after a fatal blow in a Hurricane.

Someone mentions asexual propagation techniques
        cuttings and grafts, and tissue culture methods,
or, for whatever it's worth
        clone living descendants, the headline reads
"Move over, Dolly. Make way for the Liberty Tree"
—seedlings come from scions—the legacy matters—
becomes the DNA of American history, all that "we fought for"—
        one argues, "It must be the same DNA!"
                Who is the "we" and what was "we fought?"
        another asserts, "It's a different world"
the forests have changed, the temperatures,

whole species gone north or south, these trees have no resistance
—these were trees for the liberty of white persons
　　　　—*Not so!*—men surround the scion, the clone transmits
the "best" idea we ever had—back to every state of the union.

Resistance

The Sons of Liberty trim an elm on Feb 14, 1766, "for the public good"—
the first step toward a Liberty Pole, easier to make stand, replace, and move when
soldiers chop it up (down)—like after Concord and Lex, the elm/progenitor of
the brood, fallen prey to redcoats who mocked its "last words"
in their Soliloquy of the Boston Liberty Tree:
　　"If ever there should be a shoot,
　　Spring from my venerable root,
　　Prevent, of heaven! it ne'er may see,
　　Such savage times of liberty."

The canopy spreads [what a voice does, a town crier]
while animals and birds feast and fly
　　sotto voce
oxygen and nitrogen and sugar, carried by seed
designed to withstand drought and cold
and infiltrate soil many miles away—
　　　　escaped men signing up for battle
　　[a citizen to stand his ground? What is a person who carries the seed
　　　　farther than allowed?]

///

Job Williams cuts the Boston Liberty Tree for firewood during the siege; a
more precise story anyway, *trying* to mark the boundary of a stump,
　　with the idea of *liberty's* crown and trunk, the parts easiest hauled off—
　　and after the evacuation, Liberty's Sons erect a pole beside the stump
bare and ridiculous with a floppy "Liberty cap"—
until each tree destroyed by troops gets this partial translation as a pole,
　　carried to New York, Maryland, and Delaware
　　　　at the first opportunity: contact.

"New Hampshire, hitherto immune to the contagion, now showed
signs of succumbing when the residents of little Greenland introduced the patriot
symbol on Dec 17, 1774 . . ."

Poles planted through Connecticut, and south to Savannah, GA,
where under an oak the Declaration of Independence is read:
                                        laughing, again, always laughing
        [a voice yells "Redcoats advancing!"]
Tories laugh at the "Happiness of Assembling in the open air,
        and performing idolatrous and vociferous Acts of Worship,
        to a Stick of Wood called a Liberty Pole"
                "Of high renown here grew the tree—
                The elm so dear to liberty
                This day, with filial awe, surround
                Its root, that sanctifies the ground
                And, by your fathers' spirits, swear
                The rights they left you'll not impair."

Trees and poles cross every border south to Charlestown:
"Rights! which declare, that all are free
        In person and in Property . . .
And that, when other Laws take Place,
Not to resist, wou'd be Disgrace;
Not to resist, wou'd treach'rous be,
Treach'rous to Society"
                (*On Liberty Tree*, anon.)

                        Resistance

August 14, 1765, the largest elm in Hanover Square
gets possessed with effigies, dangling *joyfully* they say
the branches *proud* with stuffed dolls
        a small group shouts Look! The royal stamp-agent Oliver, dismembered
and the devil beside him! *Let's to the man's house*
        [a tree to run? How can a tree run?]
See the real Oliver terrorized, his home hacked by boots and axes,

his furniture torched, for that "one grasp of ore"
    panting, hands on knees, he pleads
guilty, but spare the children!

a placard, bloodied, reads "liberty" and not a capillary spectacle of bark or branch
wounded with the nail, naming it *Tree* [a thing] *of Liberty* [that idea]
  [a goddess, or a snake, not the real property: an enslaved woman]
     not a tree's unseen relation of light and water, only
        loyalists, mocking it
 "consecrated as an Idol for the Mob to Worship"
while sons of the liberty-thing do it up
    [a voice wonders, does a tree have a right?]
    to *rehearse*
on beer-soaked grass; finding "more than common fruit" in the branches.

{{{}}}

November 1, 1765, Portsmouth, RI, the coffin is real, but no body:
    [*Liberty* just the name of an imaginary un-free (taxed) person]
shroud on the coffin reads: "Liberty, aged 145,"
          whose death then? a symbol's?
     taxed paper and playing cards and tea
     and colonies protecting their "institutions"—
born in depravity from a Puritan father, and now a martyr-mother,
     marchers act out their "mourning"
     a *nation, protesting* a notion,
that levy on people's purchase that poses such threat to their freedom
     (their right to own "property," the rotted fruit of their dreams)
     with the elms dragged into it, in orchards and towns
       in swamps and along the farmer's hedge,
       commons and straight on Main—no tree is mad for profit,
and yet a thirsty thing   *refrains*
    [freedom, a voice can ask: does a tree have a need for it?]
    what is the tax then? And what is the thing?

Seamstresses sew emblems: tree-flags and jargon, *do not tread on me*
    not odors and endocrine, sugars and foggy breath

not a twist of knot and phloem, sap-cycle—home for bugs and birds—
  only effigies (these with names): George Grenville and John Huske
  and straw and dolls and a ditty, hung:

> *"But if some Brethren I culd Name,*
> *Who shar'd the Crime, should share the shame,*
> *This glorious Tree tho' big and tall,*
> *Indeed would never hold 'em all."*

November 3, John Hancock hoists the meeting flag atop the "sacred elm"
calling rebels to confront the Gov'ner, himself a no-show, before they head
down
        to the boats   *singing*
Tom Paine told us the Tree was a Goddess from "the gardens above"
—and now *"King, Commons, and Lords are uniting amain*
    To cut down this guardian of ours"
fetishized, as all bought-things get, surrounded,
    a tree war-armed to *smoke out the offender,*
 branches: real; fruit: not; real signs; liberties not;
    was ever a tree an old medieval cross, suffering the ocean
    to land in a little port?
            wives, rebels running
full of "reason" and rights
initiate *"Americans"*—(a name already ef-faced, partially de-faced, *carved into*)
the order of river and ridge, and animals said to speak one language in many ways;
    a peace tree dug up and replanted by the Iroquois
over the weapons of five nations, a federation real as rain-soaked roots,
and birds bringing seeds to grow on turtle-back island
    (not on the European men's map).

Resistance

Men surround a tree, debate the problem;
some want immediate action, others more discussion;
lives are at stake here, they shout at each other
because happiness is not as it should be.

gangs of men are sent, sometimes armed soldiers, to identify
a tree, a body, a border, an idea, to surround and celebrate, or destroy,
     property
depending on its position, and what might be found there;
how fast the contagion is spreading.

/   // ///

a tree surrounded, as a natural thing is imagined—
(an idea shows what it's not, on neighboring land)
where a thing can be thought, and a thing can be cut down
these are different responsibilities
like a pole is a tree for some purposes,
         as an "is" is an "ought"
as around the pole they drunken-dance,
and people hear of it, the idea moves,
a young sapling may change history
             or leave it to die
cured by a dose which might otherwise be fatal.

//   // //

a tree surrounded by men
in their natural cover, speaking, but
             interrupting
[make this easier: here's a voice, a vector between neighbors]
         Canopy. Insects. Roots. Sapwood. (Later: a coffin.)
         A tree, a voice, going round 'til it comes around
         from the crowd, a government.
         A tree? To cross an ocean?

[The story, once sure of itself, becomes a situation]

surrounded, and coming around: *a gang of children crossing Elm*
         [A contagion dangerously close: *will you emulate us?*]
Do you remember natural *things*, children
         freely leaping, hiding, undergirding spirals of dread and doomish
     thinking,

[*children*, like that other thing, *tree*, also defined thru profitability]
children chalk tree trunks at ground-line, imagining:
a pre-dead pole, a plank cast to life,
the fear in the tremor of loved ones,
the premises: coffins pulled up hills by horses,
boat masts, lathed; furniture to be defended;
all in all, a tree already everywhere, everyone's property, yet found wanting.

Draw a tree with droplets that tiny hair roots touch,
with the action of water from one place to another, circulating
out of breath
the children draw a line, topped with a circle, just barely understanding the
water cycle.

Resistance

Across the ocean—[A tree? To cross an ocean?]
people whisper: Revolution! They lost their heads!
Was Tom Paine the vector?
or Lafayette, who stood on the stump at Essex and Washington for a good
half-hour?

Henri Gregoire: "The tree destined to become the emblem of liberty ... must
be chosen from those with long lives and, if it cannot be everlasting, at least
it should be chosen from among those trees whose life lasts several centuries."

Jacobins looking back over their shoulders, move the tree idea
to Vienne, France, 1790; destined for blood and revolution,
a voice sneers: *Why does a tree need a hat?*
a rallying cry, composed of costumes at odds,
a drunken mob
after Louis XVI tells Saint-Michel and Saint-Antoine
they may not display their freedom *arbres*—inciting a march on the
Tuileries—until midnight and the king is *forced to wear the liberty hat himself!*
resurrecting
the *mai pole* of the countryside,
pruned to its uppermost, and painted in yearly *charivari*
fixed with razors and inkwells and planted before a manor house

—the first of many raids on rich families—
[a humiliating demand: furniture and wine—the terror of neighbors]
until all *mai poles* are hacked into menacing silence
stalking, advancing, alive:
Amsterdam, 1795; Rome, 1798; then Ireland—
until not a son is born who doesn't have roots to defend.

Resistance

a tree surrounded by men in their national uniforms, fighting
interrupting 1917,
American bombs arrive in elm-wood crates
splintering, rainy piles; the war cuts deep
through tissue, forests and field
cannons through incontinence
as nurses pack dead boys for return trips home
in those same elm crates
[make this easier: here's a voice between neighbors]
Canopy. Insects. Roots. Sapwood. (Now: a coffin)
—while in Holland, a tree yellows, wilts—*it's hard to see,*
men argue, place blame in the name: Dutch Elm disease,
attacking—*without reason*—Versailles' majestic rows; Bremen,
Germany, and Bucharest, their avenues; Vienna's many parks; even Windsor
Palace stands bare—

as suddenly funerals wind along denuded Main Streets
[A battle? To cross an ocean?] our boys in the missing shadow
of the Statue of Liberty [a gift, to return?] holding up her candle—
taunting a profit-sick nation—to look at imports
men accusing; this war infects America!
a New Jersey tree yellows   *voices start counting*
New York, now Connecticut 800 trees; 6,800 one year later
Now 120,000. Now 4.5 million—*shouting*, it's the veneer
of "re-used" burl
[to make chairs, *flesh*, to cross an ocean?] those coffin boxes
sailed in from France and sold under the name "Carpathian Elm"
docked in Baltimore and Norfolk.

Resistance

The fungus invading the sapwood does not travel in wind or rain.
Only a tiny beetle ties the fungus to its hatchlings
       fly my babies, far as you can!
seek yellowing leaves! dying at night, fly at night
the men gather and rip the sapwood down the trunk—
      see the tell-tale brown—the odor of death
—before the young take their *happy liberties*
      —cut the trees and soak the stumps in kerosene—
doesn't matter: infection moves six times faster
      than shouting, recall the old soldiers!
uproot them all, cash their pay (the WPA funds the campaign)
      boots shuffling house to house
      while train and trucks feed logs along the corridors
         making forests into highways joining cities, factories
      (wetwood and slime flux, black-spot leaf—
now banned up and down the rivers, men scream out)
      plug the entrances—shut the towns!
Not enough and oh, so late—
a barn door locked after the horse has escaped.

(((○)))

Surrounding the stump, children ask: *Will all the trees be killed?*
Oh my darlings: would you rather the rot be left to run its course?
      [A rot to run?] *they laugh*
The street-tree dollar value is high, for real estate and small-town charm,
to remove infection, can't we simply prune and clear the swamps,
      so ghosts don't send up a shoot, and time can't graft a limb—
      A *voice, in panic wonders*
         birds and farmland and hedges and edges—
      the naturalists reply: *Happy news!*
Dead and dying trees make excellent nest sites
      and food sources and promote more species
—*leave the diseased and dying trees!*

Resistance

Another war gathering men to argue, call up more soldiers
　　　　interrupting the 1941 Dutch Elm Eradication Program
　　　(cutting money to care for trees, they shout
　　　　　　"Learn to live with the disease!")
and "with this world war there's no more one nation can afford!"
　　　A tree may move in the wind, *but cannot run*
　　　men surround the factories and shout, we must help
the resistance—[A resistance? To cross a road?]
Yes, the front has multiple lines—the enemy, multiple fronts
 and we can ill afford to go (not to go!)　　*to sit still*
How would a child draw it?—*arrows moving across dotted lines*
　　　broken shapes *staggering, a soldier draws a soldier out—*
　　　the passionate intimacy of killing, bite through skin
　　　parasites bite before and after battles
　　　　　　swarming and feverish
　　　mosquito swamps and broken dams—
　　　　　　bio-warfare to halt the advance.

***

　　　A molecule arrives, to prove a hero
　　　　　[a molecule? To win a battle?], from Switzerland to Florida
　　　factories buy the right to change the name
　　　mass-made, tank-sprayed, B-25s and C-47s
drop war-dividends on foreign beaches and waterways
　　　　from Italy to Saipan, kill the insects—*so troops can live*
　　　　to cross, to advance, to kill—
　　　women and children
　　　treaties and surrendering, the wars
—known to be very persistent in the environment—
　　　accumulate in fatty tissues,
and travel long distances in the upper atmosphere.

Resistance

High-pressure spray soaks the foliage, the roots
    drink and soak what the molecule protects, the healthy tree,
    the disease travels as far west as Colorado,
    south as Virginia—*which disease? which trees?*
    houseflies, mosquitoes, and now the bark beetle;
    develop resistance so *more is never enough* [is freedom a property?]
and the mayors for the 4th of July celebrations
    parade   up and down, sanitizing citizens,
      the children,
    against *communist infiltrators, against agitators*
    but mostly for *laws* that white-wash the red-white-blue
    tree-lined parade route *in the glare of missing elms,* and remember
      who fought
      and for what
      and ignore the rot in the root
    a mean information field (coming around)
an infection-probability field (goes around)
    as new laws and control methods develop.

"There can't be controlled use of something uncontrollable,"
someone whispers, *demanding to be here, everyone fights*
    the men surround the lake, debate the civil rights
    the silence suddenly
of neighbors and strangers, stopped by crude trespass
    of whites-only places
    around Lake Michigan,
    where tiny plankton have 3 ppm of the chemical DDT, whitefish have
3 ppm, herring gulls have 80 ppm in muscle, and 1,925 ppm in fat//with magni-
fication up the food chain: osprey, falcons, eagles—

Resistance

Scientists surround a young body, surprised at liquids invalidating
    borders where parasites stare across the face,
      and every thirty seconds a child dies, a mosquito born

2017: 450,000 people of an infected 219 million
[a disease, to cross the ocean?] *not so fast,* the White-man warns
shouts: "It's going to be man or mosquito!"
Shouts him down: "DDT has saved more human lives than anything else
ever combined!" Others *respond*: it's "a chemical compound of extinction"
– not viable! someone *begs*: human death from malaria at an all-time high!
Dominoes topple in the film, and a chain reaction in a red-stained dish,
spatially diffuses: "this is how vectors spread" in a mathematical model—
well, a child, lifeless, still loved, loses the shadow, a self-same shape
that once resisted
collapse, cell walls hold back
like trees withstand, bend in wind, keep their place—
until something breaks, until invaders
until ignorance (ignoring)
[make this easier: here's a voice, a cry between neighbors]

Resistance

In a London lab: gene-altered mosquitos self-destruct in eleven generations—
he explains: the gene-drive infiltrates
larvae, leaves no place for mutations
like the ones that escaped the "genetic trap" of previous engineering
so—in the wild—whole populations would crash, babies first?
Yes, *It's never been tried, let's try it!*
someone replies, *a natural thing, the freedom, can harm*
Dr. Esvelt of MIT: "The known harm of malaria greatly outweighs
every possible ecological side-effect that has been posited to date, even if all
of them occurred at once"
others argue, *ad hominem*—lives are weighed;
small and large, larva and adult—surrounded by natural (national) weapons—
flies surround a body and claim it for their children,
suggesting an attack on the problem
yelling and accusing
feeding and sustaining
          ◌   ◌   ◌   ◌

Someone mentions malaria nets, mis-used to fish the swamps
and lakes of Zambia, Nigeria, Mozambique, Congo, Uganda—

"Along with protecting sleeping families!"
Feeding the children comes first, a voice yells back,
even if the nets are so fine as to take all the eggs and baby fish up in them?
      Reed baskets look silly next to a mosquito net!
You will destroy the fish, and then what will you eat anyway?
The nets save lives! Today to eat, tonight to sleep!
A super fine sieve, laden with pesticide, designed in Europe, manufactured in
Asia, folded into steel containers, shipped across the oceans, trucked across
the deserts to villages given out—since 2000, malaria deaths have been cut
by half. But spread across a world where nothing is one thing, the nets are
soccer balls and funeral shrouds, and chicken coop, spreading insecticide
and poisoning the fish drying in the sun, the fish which the children eat—
      surrounded on all sides, the boxes contain so many little liberties
      silent in so many languages
      a dead baby holding the thriving bodies of billions
because "artimisinin"—the latest wonder drug—lost its effectiveness in
Western Cambodia—the parasite's resistance to the drug then moving 1,500
miles to the border between Myanmar and India—*mosquitos can't be
detained*—like all "contagious contact"—
      fancy words for political change: *"mirror systems of emulation"*
         like nationalism to bordering nations
         modeling effects
[*an effect to cross, to trend?*]
         as people change their freedom
   through *interdependent states—not autonomous actors*
in other words, no national "hard shell" exists
         all lives stand permeable to irresistible forces—
including democratic norms, insect larvae, or autocratic *repression*
      [a tool to cross a line?] [a molecule to invade?]
         as governments transition to more or less freedom,
with or without idealists *debating*, in response to their borders
the "neighbor effect" (*like the blood-brain barrier, someone suggests*)
demanding immediate action, or more discussion
lives are at stake, they shout at each other
               as an "is" is an "ought"
as many countries *cascade* from Free to Not
      one says: "freedom is not a simple task"

[censorship! to close the gaps?] *going around, coming around*
shifting from Not Free to Partially Free, burning the furniture first
then the house, humiliating the hosts,
killing the messengers, guests, and blaming random events
that seem to increase the likelihood of other events
a "Contagious Poisson" or, how autocratic states spread like fire, or fungus—
[what does rebellion look like in a forest?]

Resistance

Men surround, again, a tree, to lose their wits
        to drink their brains, to lean against the trunk
    to drag a boy over, and beat a man
    [two names, to cross out, to not map]
    a mob enjoys a picnic on the designated day
        yelling, *lemme see!* at others
    laughing
  applauding *pop'lar justice*
    —for looking wrong, for looking
    [a right? a look? a vector between neighbors?]
    a tale as old as time—[names, as old as forget]
 go on down to the hanging tree:
to *Gallows Hill* where the witches hung
to *Hangman's Elm* in Washington Square Park,
to the *Bur Oak* in Tulsa, where the Creek chief swung
to Centerville, Texas or the *Old Hanging Oak* in Houston
    and thousands of other names on the repressed page
  of justice, with its back turned, scissors in hand
    drunk and asleep—
the men surround, some to dig and some to cover up
 climb and fix the ropes, to twice hang
    the boy and beat the man, double-burned, triple-named
for resisting "natural conditions"—natural law and
the way some get told *what's exactly what*
  through the phases of violence, percentages and rules
    walking, breathing, laboring, looking
      a broken branch becomes kindling

or the branch holds foreign weight
　　[a chair to own its floor? A tree its soil?]
　　　　　　For the rain to gather, for the wind to suck
　　　　　　For the sun to rot, for the tree to drop
well, no, a branch would break, a tree can heal
as white supremacists know full well
　　to burn the picnic lawn
　　　　　[a cross, to cross a lawn?]
can't burn the trouble out—"what's ours by God!"
　　enforced, the sill of the house that holds it up
　　a tree takes many sides, holds many shapes
　　　　　　For the sun to rot, for the tree to drop
　　　　　　Here is a strange and bitter crop
　　unfree as work unpaid
　　argues the sun—debates the winds
　　don't ever walk past, whisper:　　*keep running,*
　　　　　　　　　　　　　　　　　don't walk near that tree
　　recruited for the shade
　　　　　　　　　　children flee, all children, run
　　　　　　　　　　　　outrun the disease
　　　　　　　　and take the seed
where no markers grow, seedlings and saplings, enduring memory
　　in the memory of the tree on Herndon Street
where young Klan thugs hung a boy
　　"Like Trees, Walking"—on what now is Michael Donald Ave.

Resistance

monologue, from inside a tree-costume:

To will one's limbs to lengthen, to stretch one's reach as if by magic, to open one's throat, to lift the chin, to wake early and nap surreptitiously, to seem never to give an inch or a mile . . . A fight leaves a wound vulnerable, yet in the end I was tall, not rotten, eaten, not surrendered, yet one would immediately cut me down; wrong place, wrong in some towns, right in others, and burn the stump or prop me up, I'm no fool, the leaves that drop protect the root, and I am deformed as are all who struggle for light.

Resistance

Boston Herald, October, 1966:
The city's only commemoration of the Liberty Tree is a grimy plaque three stories
above what is now the intersection of Essex and Washington.
Covered with bird droppings, the plaque is equally obscured by a hamburger sign.
  This site, "where America was born," is left out of guidebooks.
  The governor promises a park with "the largest elm tree that can be
transported and is resistant to Dutch elm disease"—
   Is that really where America was born? someone asks—
  the tree never arrives, but a small plate in the sidewalk says
   Sons of Liberty, 1766; Independence of the Country, 1776

///   ///

Other trees recruited along the way, standing in the forest we can't name:

 A poplar in Maryland marks the Chesapeake region declared by
   Europeans;
 The Treaty Elm where William Penn in 1683 concluded peace;
 Hartford, 1687, the Charter Oak, where the colonial charter was buried for
   safekeeping;
 Newport Liberty Tree, given in 1766
   for "public liberty in all Times and Ages forever hereafter";
 Norwich, CT dedicates a Liberty Tree, 1767;
 New York Common had a pine-tree of Liberty, cut down by soldiers;
 Providence, RI dedicates a great elm, 1768, with a platform in the boughs
   for speeches:
   "that Liberty which our forefathers sought out, and found under Trees,
   and in the Wilderness"—

THE HEALTH OF MY STREAM OR THE (MOST) PATHETIC FALLACY

—

Zhuangzi said, "Let's go back to your original question, please.
You asked me *how* I know what fish enjoy—
so you already knew that I knew it when you asked the question.
I know it by standing here beside the Hao."

1.

A wobbly line on the brave old bridge shows where a terrible storm in 1982 caused the once-shy river to wash out trees, vineyards, and the lower village.

A few towns over, ancient cliff-houses plunged into another panicked river. People died.

Consequently, "measures" were taken: rocks cemented down, bed deepened, loose 'debris' cleared.

2.

It is worth the perfect cliché of the land beside it (staid old barn, cheerful vineyard, and majestic olive trees beneath limestone cliffs . . .).

It is worth the extra line on the survey map (though I'm not sure it added money-value).

It is impenetrably, fundamentally, entangled.

Visibly obscured.

Fresh-water springs from Alp-fed aquifers flow joyfully into it—from pipes, from catch-basins, and from village fountains that have slaked thirsts, saying: "here's all the water you need!"

It was only of faint concern during the industrious life of the stone barn— amiable donkeys warming the loft; moisture causing lime scale to leech from the walls.

3.

With the barn transformed into a house, collapsing hill shored up, spiritless terrain planted, run-off redirected, town water and sewer accorded, certificate of occupancy granted – with all this accomplished, there could be meals and showers, and a toilet, and an agreeable bed for sleeping.

Cicadas' daytime rioting recedes at dark, as the river-voice rises, insistent as an impatient question, close inside the head, behind awake eyes.

Is it a healthy stream? I didn't think to ask.

4.

Without irrigation, the dry season brutalizes plants who can't reach groundwater beneath the stingy clay. But *owning* a riverbank, by right I can use what water I can get. From a hose installed with pegs near the bridge, and from the silty pump: lavender, trumpet vines, roses, star-jasmine, wisteria, oleander, viburnum, sage, apricot, cherry, and plums fruiting and flowering; butterfly bushes and bay and borders of spunky wildflowers.

From these: butterflies, bees, wasps, hummingbird moths. Wood pigeons gliding from high oaks to lower ones. The occasional heron. The rarer eagle. Curious gangs of jays. Carefree yellow songbirds. Industrious lines of ants and geckos and shaded scorpions. The sunning mantis, the long-horned beetle, the wolf-spiders in their cave-webs. Twilight swarms with gnats and mosquitos, hunted by dragonflies, swallows, and finally bats, outlasting the remainder of church bells, until the moon rises and the garrulous river rejoins a sky transfixed by stars.

5.

Invisibility nags.

Audibility teases. Always right near me, what I can't see.

Tease, tempt, taunt, dare? Sounds blind.

The river roars, yet stays unseen.

Impetuously, I decide to clear and cut the length of the riverbank, especially the prolific nettle and bramble. Save the healthy poplar, oak, a few wild box, and one small expanse of blackberry, minding its splurge of August fruit.

6.

An espied stream looks smaller and narrower than it sounds. I peer and mark it along a hundred meters, and where my eyes go, so turbulences and gravel-runs put a face to bubbling jumps and falls. Here in plain view, the river breathes and rumbles and laughs, and now I see catches and swirls, rushing, dawdling, while dragonflies patrol out of sight and zoom back. Water-hoppers stick, moss adorns bald rocks, and I had heard it faintly, but now I locate a spring, prattling down the overgrowth on the opposing bank. A single hornet and a snake dart sideways.

The sunlight falls where shade was resting. I commission a "secret garden" just above the high-water mark on the grasses, but below the level of the vineyard: a rusty bench on a patch of gravel.

7.

I can sit beside the river now and see things.

A shadow turns and disappears in the deepest pool, where the flow slugs and sunlight can't touch, just downstream of ornery rocks in a hindrance of waterfall.

More shadows move. Agitated eddies, and the mirroring light, protect them from uninvited eyes.

8.

Polarized glasses reveal an array of mud-colored fish, and I feel caught in a sudden enraptured vigil; rich with time to spend. Here to purchase their belonging, mine, I haunt the bench. Vigilant.

One fish lurks most of the day beneath an overhang. Smaller ones slip over a gravel rise between the obscure pool and a smaller one downstream. A mysterious dark one rushes the little ones as they enter the deep. He scares them off, retreats. Several smaller fish worship directly below the trickle, hovering.

July, August, a summer of insistent heat, no humidity, foregone ground, brown but for the drought-tolerant greens in mid-view: olives, cyprus, sage, rosemary, broom, oak, poplar, pine. Every day I join the happy fish, following their movements, the insects, the grasses, the skirting hastiness of the waterfall's repeating, the languid way we all persist in the single-minded flow for hours and hours. I am moved; a becoming that feels more like myself than I've felt in a long time—in love with a life that has fish in it.

9.

A few days before I'm set to leave, a blast convulses from the innocuous trickle, a rancid bomb in the water, reeking of excrement; fish scatter into a chaos of dissolved paper, weird strings, plastic. Foam the color of overcooked vegetables, *in danger*, wherever that is. After a few minutes, the horror un-clots downstream. The fish vanished.

Night resolves. I cannot sleep in it. I am nauseous and sobbing. Yet the fish are back the next morning. Joyful staring until dark by their side.

10.

A repeat explosion a day later. I get waders and go in to look.

The once-calm trickle now tirades from a broken pipe jutting from the slope, coating the rocks at the river in something slimy that stinks of over-rich waste.

I investigate a new horse barn across the way. A shack used by local men to carve and cook up wild boar in hunting season. Road work done. Electric lines dug. Straight up the steep bank, a town water-pump lets farmers fill their tanks. An open grate: would caravans empty their septics? Or pipes from the upper village, centuries old, ignored?

I visit the town secretary, describing the problem. I fear that indicating there are fish, someone will fish them, this is a rural place after all, where pilfering seems the rule. Truffles, wild asparagus, mushrooms, fruits, olives, nuts. Possession is only presence; I'm part-time present.

There is a woman with an old house not on the modern system. The town will look into it.

11.

I must leave my bench and go back to work, though I hold in mind: my fish, their daily circuits, their daring forays, the way they hang steadfast in strong current, in shadow, even their strange attraction to the mystery-pipe's secrets.

12.

"The fish are gone"—emails the one person I confided in before I left. "There were huge storms."

Rushing to the bench when I get back in March, decoding the colors distraught in swirling water, the tails of branches that look for all the world like fish shadows, I pass a whole day, two, in despair. A third fitful night, sad waking loss of appetite. Panic. Nausea. I didn't realize how much they had come to mean. Yet, in all my time in their company (was I their company?) I hadn't once thought to figure out who they were.

I expand photos, try to remember their markings. I decide they are brown trout. The range makes sense. The kind of stream.

I read: they prefer to hide, come out to "lie" in a favorite spot, in riffles or downstream of fallen logs, where bugs and edible things float slowly. They can be territorial, but share limited spaces, especially with younger fish. They prefer a certain temperature for oxygenating water, otherwise they wait where it's cool, deeper, shadier, under carved banks, safely out of bird's-eye views. They dig reds for their babies in the shallow gravel transition between pool and riffle, in even flow. Sometimes they leap for insects, change color with their emotions, camouflage to the stream bed. They themselves polarize light, and, focusing from each eye independently, take in every direction at once.

Those most keen to kill them appear to possess the most expertise: "the wariest and wiliest opponent a river angler can face."

Finally, on my last day, a shadow, and another, and at twilight I see two medium-sized fish in the smaller pool. I take video and photos, overjoyed at my amazing stream, the living miracle, joyous waters, and myself the luckiest person in the entire world.

13.

In mid-May another unreasonable spring storm pushes 30 cm of rain across dry ground, driving fast tributaries as runoff, ravaging dirt and gravel through the narrow riverbed. The smaller pool fills in; the deep pool's outwash greys in silt. I worry, pacing, the fish evacuated, shadow-less, injured, or worse—

they are not here—how could they be? Their small pool and favorite trickle swept away.

An unchecked impulse gets me in waders, with shovel and rake. It's just one pool. It's just a little stream. Certainly I can rake out gravel from around the small pool rock, like a child plays with sand at the beach, working with the pushy water to dig it back out.

I scour the field for medium-sized rocks, drop them around the pool as a barrier. Watch the water detour around them. Hopeful.

14.

In early June, a third unusually wet storm covers what I dug, steals the added rocks, and leaves more gravel and silt than before. I cry with frustration, then spend the night listening to the keening waterfall. It's supposed to be the dry season, but it's still raining as I wait for any sign of returning life. A dark curl in the deep pool is a figment of bramble.

I attempt another fix, but this time more purposeful, make myself stronger in waders with a rake and shovel. Clearly the gravel dumped beyond the deep pool has made the channel too wide and shallow for fish to swim up. So first I sling silt to the banks, sending dirty swirls downstream. Then I rake gravel into a center island, inventing channels on both sides that might—hopefully—deepen with the corralled flow. Since I read that fish like to 'lie' where there are current seams, I try to create one.

15.

A commotion reveals a heron flapping awkwardly from my bench into the taller trees. I run, but the bird's faster. Does this predator mean the fish are back? Or was the heron also checking, hoping? My hand-dug gravel island suddenly looks like a self-serve counter. It takes two days, but I shovel it away, towering piles on either bank. My hands are calloused, bleeding, and the river 'sort of' looks like it did before. Which before? I don't know.

16.

Heat of July, the sun unforgiving. Every grain of gravel has miraculously disappeared from the stream banks, and the wide, shallow run has grown even wider and shallower. The small pool I dug is entirely gone. The deep pool, however, seems deeper.

Day after day, no fish. Despondent branches, tokens of light. I visit the bench less, linger less each time. Without the fish, I can't love it here. Their lives made sense of the whole place.

17.

I mope up to the village secretary who tells me that they did finally work on the old lady's sewer. It's true: there are moments when the flow from the pipe grows stronger, but the stench doesn't return. No more paper or plastic. Problem, and fish, gone.

Humidity weirdly high in August; the moist desert air pushing up, cold air from the mountains bearing down, producing violent, early thunderstorms and 40 cm of rain in a few hours, sending boulders galloping downstream, threatening the bridge. When I emerge from the house between sheets of rain and look around, I see rocks occupying new places, including one blocking the pipe-trickle entirely. Even the overhanging banks have filled in.

The next morning: rake and shovel and pull some of that new gravel out . . . it drifts downstream . . . but the flow across this width is now too weak to re-carve the overhanging bank. If fish anywhere have survived, they will not come back to this spot. Bleak abyss of the deep pool offers nothing; it is practically gone.

18.

My remaining days, I avoid the shameful bench, the river rushing high and smugly now with the added floodwater. A smell of wet clay, totally unusual for end of summer. Once or twice, I think I see a shadow beckoning, perhaps a large fish survives somewhere secret where the storms didn't disturb her.

19.

I ask my neighbor, tentatively, whether people ever fish in this stream. Well, they stock it down near town in spring, he says, but those trout never make it very far. Certainly not up here.

But aren't there trout here?

No . . . there are chub, like there . . . he points to a pool near the bridge. Three or four shadows circle. We move to the railing. Are those my fish?

Those are *chub*, he repeats. They aren't so sensitive to pollution, runoff, chemicals from the vineyards. This stream is not so healthy, he laughs—though if more people like you buy up land and protect it, it might come back.

I hope so, I whisper, though hope feels weak and stupid.

20.

An entire galaxy of expert "hydrologists" and "stream managers" say that a healthy stream holds a variety of vegetation, aquatic life, and riparian zones and floodplains. Keeping the shores rich with native plants provides nesting and roosting places, overhang, shade, and root systems for stability. A healthy stream has tangled roots and tree limbs in it. Channels should meander, flow apart, rejoin, with abundant pools, undercut banks, boulders and fallen trees.

Riprapped banks cause erosion downstream. Cleaning the stream takes away critical habitat for insects, fish, birds, amphibians. Engineering a stream to flow in a straight uniform channel is to degrade it. Landowners are part of the stream's life, up and down, affecting each other.

To maintain a healthy stream, they say you have to understand the watershed, the overland flow, the groundwater table, the rainfall patterns. Watershed also determines the quality of life for fish, for example, who don't simply exist in one isolated stretch. Streams must provide cool spots, and abundant oxygen through fallen logs and rocks that mix air and water, and lots of riffle areas.

Most importantly, the stream's course changes as channels shift in storms, and runs and riffles adjust to flow and current, move in predictable ways, their serpent-like energy carving out one side and then the other. Other patterns repeat: waterfall, pool, riffle, and run . . . it's how the flow must operate. Dropping rocks where there needed to be outflow, a riffle, and then a run, is nonsensical. A healthy stream reshapes, as riparian zones and floodplains absorb flood energy so that steep or sparsely vegetated banks don't erode. Too-steep banks also force water too fast. Having engineers come in and straighten channels, or put boulders along to fortify them, end up doing the opposite, and ruins the habitat in the process.

Places with infrequent rains have the worst oil and hydrocarbon runoff. Air pollution comes from rainwater, storm-water runoff, local vineyards, farming, traffic. Silt and clay clog the gravel where fish and insects breed, a problem called "embeddedness."

One expert suggests having a "stream vision" that you share with your family and neighbors. They say that streams can heal themselves, given time and no interference.

21.

Would it change the understanding of the stream, the fish, my obsession with rakes and rocks, if I revealed that just before clearing the banks and spotting the fish, I suffered a betrayal of the most devastating kind? Would more story inform the flow of it, make it gain or lose power, render it all banal? Would more information change the question of where the stream begins and ends?

They say that to be god-like is to know space and time all at once. And yet, even in the first garden, where God was omniscient and none of the creatures had knowledge of good or evil, tricks and betrayals unfolded that no one seemed to have a handle on.

22.

The waterfall entirely caved this spring, leaving only one flat shallow pool with a long run leading to the riffles. Still, fish dart in and out of re-cut overhangs, feed in the seams, and hang out in the quieter flow.

A heron swoops down from the north, lands gracefully in the water. As I run from the house, she lifts her wings and flaps downstream with her catch. By mid-summer, most fish are gone.

At dinner, someone suggests installing a painted heron decoy on the bank. Someone else says put bigger rocks in the river so the waterfall will dig the deep pool again. My neighbor laughs, just hang a net across the entire stream from side to side!

23.

In more than one country, rivers have been granted the right of personhood, in the recognition that they possess the imagination and sacred feeling of those who count on them.

IN THE HIGH COURT OF UTTARAKHAND AT NAINITAL
Writ Petition (PIL) No. 126 of 2014

Mohd. Salim . . . . . . **Petitioner** *Versus* State of Uttarakhand & others . . . **Respondents**

17. All the Hindus have deep Astha in rivers Ganges and Yamuna and they collectively connect with these rivers. Rivers Ganges and Yamuna are central to the existence of half of Indian population and their health and well-being. The rivers have provided both physical and spiritual sustenance to all of us from time immemorial. Rivers Ganges and Yamuna have spiritual and physical sustenance. They support and assist both the life and natural resources and health and well-being of the entire community. Rivers Ganges and Yamuna are breathing, living, and sustaining the communities from mountains to sea.

---

18. The constitution of Ganges Management Board is necessary for the purpose of irrigation, rural and urban water supply, hydro power generation, navigation, industries. There is utmost expediency to give legal status as a living person/legal entity to Rivers Ganges and Yamuna r/w Articles 48-A and 51A(g) of the Constitution of India.

19. Accordingly, while exercising the *parens patriae* jurisdiction, the Rivers Ganges and Yamuna, all their tributaries, streams, every natural water flowing with flow continuously or intermittently of these rivers, are declared as juristic/legal persons/ living entities having the status of a legal person with all corresponding rights, duties, and liabilities of a living person in order to preserve and conserve Rivers Ganges and Yamuna. The Director of NAMAMI Gange, the Chief Secretary of the State of Uttarakhand, and the Advocate General of the State of Uttarakhand, are hereby declared persons in loco parentis as the human face to protect, conserve, and preserve Rivers Ganges and Yamuna and their tributaries. These Officers are bound to uphold the status of Rivers Ganges and Yamuna and also to promote the health and well-being of these rivers.

20. The Advocate General shall represent at all legal proceedings to protect the interest of Rivers Ganges and Yamuna.

21. The presence of the Secretary, Ministry of Water Resources, River Development & Ganges Rejuvenation is dispensed with.

22. Let a copy of this order be sent by the Registry to the Chief Secretary of the State of Uttarakhand forthwith.

PATIENTS

***

Then, it was time to practice dying—a Buddha in slow-wave sleep,
weak against the synchronous pull of the crowd
      (their last offering: a meal, then pain
            tasted – refused)
   mind the mind
walking the last six miles to *Kusinara.*

And a nauseous hovering at the ceiling,
a tent reducing space-time to vomit-colored walls
and a plastic tray with a mind on it—
     he is the most important one, and now he's leaving
     I won't let you, someone cries
—and the Buddha gave Ananda the elephant's look.

(breathing)
(not breathing)

***

Train for confusion and old age.
A bed attached to the wall, and a wall-mounted tv.
Dirty floors and mauve curtains, the hospital forces
confusion, says "reach up" and then bad for reaching up.

Confusion says wake up and sleep.
The bending down and the bad for bending down.
The saying "sit" and the "why are you sitting there!"
The situation of being in the charge of order, the order for the direction, the overall authority, the otherwise inversion of the orders. Write the letter and wait. Why did you write the letter and wait? Don't say anything. Why didn't you say anything? Try to unfold the map and step on it. Wait a few days. I told you to do it the next day.

Patience. In the lion's posture on the right side.
To be host, guest, stranger, enemy; to derive from the Latin, *hostis*. A hostile welcome in a house of illness, hospitality, welcome, to the refuge of birth and death.

***

543 BCE—flowers and birds gather in monk's robes. In the lion's posture the Buddha reclines on his right side, his mind a perfect mirror. The pains from Cunda's generous meal radiate from the gut. Mara enters. Another old age might be less prepared. Mara would like to empty the trash.

Patience.

Empty the trash. A mind unravels by night, as hands from unseen experts dump brains into buckets. Horror pulls the curtain: life just enough to die from; hospital cords, intravenous ports—Mara offers an open pen. Stay. Sign.

Three months ago an old Buddha announced she was dying.
The little ones flocked, dying in a rush of jokes, she's only joking!
I will let go at the timely hour, she says, and that is that.
May all enemies be ridiculous.
Mara came to nurse me, but I said I would make no final hold on self-preservation, and no final craving for my life. Like an old cart fastened with weak string, only be a refuge unto yourself. These ninety-three years make the body frail. Three months hence and I will utterly pass.

Mara comes to the powder-pink room; seduces the will by presenting a nurse.

(breathing)
(not breathing)

Then specialists and "hold still" and bad for not keeping moving.
Run, stop there, don't go one step, hurry up, stand still. The right side, the heart is open. And then "listen!" but you don't hear anything. Be the puppet and don't be a puppet, submitting to one more needle when the signs of dying are full, there is no reason to force, though forcing will be pushed; the carts, cups, Mara trained on this, one day's window, the frictionless turn of
     the wheel, the needling—
You give up your feet, your voice, your hands.
You give up plans, time, your season. And all the photos
     which will be badly labeled. You give up labeling.
To finish the archive means sorting.
She gives it up, and the photos fall into the corridor, into trash cans.
She once took photos of a war-torn world, destroyed by air, for all that
     "remembering"—
and then bad for holding on to remembering.

***

Then, a young Buddha announced she was pregnant, in a city of foreign nausea—eat against death, they instruct, the hospital meals going down, a dose question, she refuses as the nausea refuses, but can't avoid the hospitality of care because there's a food part, and a terrible food part, feeding what cannot die—swallow, sit up, one two three. There's postponing one thing until they change the order of things, but still reorient or compare awakenings, or just quinine and something in the toilets which never belonged to you. Adjustment of medication remains likely, but why adjust medications? Having visited the old and dying, she knows: death diet, birth diet, sucking reflexes, the wet and desperate mouth for moisture. Who is a baby? When is a baby? Organs shut, don't shut up, and require everything; the hospital makes promises, empties them.

Propped on the left side, told to stay,
blood to the gathering, a birth takes months
following the tiny floating body parts,

and dreams of white elephants entering
would have made a nice story, but no dreams come without sleep,
in a hospital only flushing, nausea, cords and Mara, who stalks the foot of the
bed with whispers of headaches and death, a nurse of books says it's okay to
    die of books, she says,
but the child makes me afraid: to leave something of life, growing?
an unfinished book needs me, and makes me afraid. I haven't said what I was
    saying.
I'm not done reading what life is writing, at autumn out the window.
Mara pulls the curtain back, says, "Pass on."
The practiced know Mara's tricks. "No thanks, I'll take three more months."

***

The Buddha hung his bed in two trees and went for a last drink from the river. In silence, he refused food and other stuff. His visitors' grief consumed their minds, they tangled their hair and withdrew to the side. They believed in their thoughts, their needs.
Dying is active work. To be born. But one can become tired of working.

A great earthquake an hour later.

(breathing)
(not breathing)

Another swallow, the nurse wakes her and removes blood. All at the same time. Left-lying, broken clock, blood draw, ideas separate and go. Practice getting lost; practice not arguing with dreams.

Patience.

Visitors feel a rush, beat their heads, sobbing, offering the most fragrant pastries and pleasures and gifts, and she continues refusing. Everyone needs the dying to take something. Tears arise. You have to feed the life inside you; a nurse removes more visitors to a pained cage. "Take this." Why would anyone take that? Refusal is peace.

Then, strange and suddenly, death sits, talking quietly, and eyes focus, and names remembered and swallowing calmly. For a moment, hands under control, more sitting up and swallowing some lunch, and a few smiles and a picture glued together.

Look, a window beyond the curtains, and outside a season, with people walking. Speak gently to the window, let it know it's a window and you are some wind. Reassure the wind of the window. Resume the active training, to touch food to the mouth. A map of wind and heat.

But the grey elephant says: Do not distract the dying from dying. Die harder. Faster. And so the nausea returns with nurses floating in it. The force of the left side, the bad right, those colored tubes and threads load the room into a circus. For what are there except elephants along the entire hallway? Greys and finally white, and yet not a living elephant to give the final look because in all the zoos and hospitals there are no living elephants left—

And there is a moment when you are not the patient or near the patient and it is like sanity. It's an offering and it's murder. In the disguise of nursing, in the disguise of the labor which is dying, rebirth is less training, an unfinished sit-up. The not-thinking look, she pushes away, and the "don't give up your very last word"—as she chooses to become fully animal.

(breathing)
(not breathing)

Why did someone open the window?
It's in the book. It's written that there are a lot of pages without windows.
And that someone will open a word to close the door.
Because she can fly like swallows out of the word.
There's "listen closely" and then the misunderstanding.
Despite the repetition each time, an animal nested in animals, testing animals inside animals connected by colored tubes and screens, shows them alive and running.

"There is someone in the bed, and I want to get back in. Help me, I am not in my room, and this is not my number," she means, can she have her map back? The box of pictures?
All this hard pain feeds another wolf. The world-wolf cries when it cannot find its pack. The world-wolf is her other side, lying on the right.

Madame, what are you doing over there?
The sight of other extinctions would shock.
Gestate the memory of no-more-births;
that's the true death; she shouldn't be standing up. Nurse calls in help.
Morpheus always playing with shapes of babies:
do not try to reorient reality; there will be no more babies,
the maternity ward is the hospice in a hospital zoo.

Mara has brought some friends.

There's the training to refuse the offerings, and visitors howling and slashing themselves. Don't scream at the dying to "sit up." The outside animal may die to save the inside animal. She has long given up swallowing, but swallows in the sky respond to the wind like a baby. A voice is love and she responds; hearing being the last sense. Push down the tongue, massage the throat. Practice dying in sleep or you'll just keep waking up. Birth, she reminds them, has lost its memory, too.

Maybe I'll just be spontaneous, she says, and takes Mara's hand.

(breathing)

Do not distract. The hand a cold bone. More visitors come after breakfast and offer everything the patient liked: Magazines. Mints. Apricots. They hold themselves up: "Don't you love us?" The Tathagata refuses the offerings and the visitors cut themselves with knives and withdraw to the side.

Don't scream at the dying. A new nurse comes close, impatient with medicine. Sit up now, *un, deux, trois*. She has long given up counting, but responds to the spoon like a baby. A voice is love and she responds. Pain is an echo of laughter, Monsieur, please step away. Step close, push down the tongue, finger the throat. Breathing will be a sign that death is close, when it runs wild and collapses for a long time.

(not breathing)

Accidents are wet and whole organs release and are lost, float off, or harden. Bring them back to the changing bed, but don't change her dress, not yet, these soft liquid moments that smell tenser than the past, waste. Visitors offer to confess. Lying on the left, on the right. Birth could fail. Death never fails. Perfect asymmetry.

Run from the fire and wait for it. Carry the water and spill it.

Left-lying for the right to pass something through: a future.
Right-lying for abdicating. Block the right nostril, head on the right hand.

There are periods of no breathing, even up to 45 seconds.

The pulse-sensor, the beeping lights. Nurses head over heels. The baby is startled and shaken awake. Nurses trained in holding and feeding babies do not work with the elderly. Doctors say nothing when asked how close death is, or plan for birth—What will happen first? What will happen next? What are you doing with all that sleep if not practicing not waking?

And the Buddha gave Ananda the elephant's look.

***

To laugh may be the last dignity, the last world we can share. Ananda enters the tent with the visitors. Manjushri and Ananda describe intense colored lights flowing from the Tathagata's facial orifices. A final display of one who, utterly awake, never wakes again.

Hearing that hearing is the last sense to quit the body, the visitors rush to yell at the corpse.

Out the window more swallows gather. An echo stumbles blindly through the woods, the surprise hallucination, empty clatter, Narcissus reborn, homeless friend of a lost "I love you."

I love you, says everyone's favorite patient; shift nurse, shift, sit up, and swallow. All gurgling sounds; rattles and blankets. Death has the same exact toys.

Don't startle, don't yell at the dying. Don't disturb the vessel preparing for birth. The animal's new interests are way past food. Sucking is first to come and last to go, as the wet cotton entices lips, and the outbreath takes too long. Train in being helpless. Soft foods first. Soft food last and turn the bed-bound body, but not at the end. Turn the baby through slow motions of the mother.

***

She screams she isn't frightened by a clock with 12 hours marked, the hours cause the hours, the minutes, the minutes. Twelve o'clock is caused by 11 o'clock, and 11 by 10, even 1 o'clock is caused by 12 o'clock and 4 o'clock by 9 o'clock. The way away from the clock is the way away from this room, at any minute a chance for freedom. "The brain is as much in the dark as any other part of the body." The nurse removes what she can of reminders.

One last bite, it won't be touched. A few sucks of juice and not a touch of juice.

Then venerable Ananda leaned against the doorpost and wailed: "I am still but a learner, and still have to strive for my own perfection. But, alas, my Master, who was so compassionate towards me, is about to pass away!"

Every door does not start with knocking; the teacher returns: "I've lost my glasses!" followed by a torrent of noun possessions. Nurses searching. Hold a hand up. And not there. Why are you raising your hand? To the shadow. Make sense and refuse calling names, they caution, until suddenly it's *we found them!* The shattered glasses are found that she no longer uses because she's already blind.

Do not lament! Hasn't she taught that beloved things come apart?

(breathing)

It all comes down to what we say and do for the elephants.

(not breathing)

Then an enormous earthquake.

"Please stay! O please stay . . . ," the visitors plead.

When death moved to the hospital, so did birth; crawled into the bed and lay on the left, on the right, and the next thing you hear will be the beds pushed closer together.

The elephants knew. They saved their babies from the mud. They tried to save them every time. They mourned and walked and ran. When they encountered the crumbled hospital the clocks had stopped. The nurses calmly trying to evacuate.

IRRATIONAL/SITUATION

—

1.

Consider Hippasus, long ago in southern Italy, a Greek diligently making his name among Pythagoras's remaining gang. Did he see the beauty in his cohort's slogans, or the perfection of simple geometry where numbers glow (the *arche* in ratios of solid agreement)?

Hippasus, perhaps a lover of roundness, of a square, of the polygons and crystals that mirrored his natural world, was filled sometimes with merriment but also (perhaps) with little patches of dread. Shaded, shadowed, bothered, did this unlucky Hippasus sense that the impossible had infected the estate?

Pythagoras's gang assumed that all angles (of things, disputes) should be orderable, reducible (one question, one answer, one story.) They liked pairs of rules and sides (of arguments, shapes) that could perfect each other through ratios of integers. But this was not always to be. Reducing to absurdity shows that the diagonal of a square with the measure of 1 produces incommensurable sides that are both even and odd. The square root of 2, the hypotenuse of the subsequent triangle (the diagonal of that ill-behaved square), thereby became the first *irrational*, a number uncontainable, spinning off magnitude from the divinity of Number, producing a decimal that wouldn't repeat and wouldn't ever end.

Only death would stop it, or so they thought, as they tossed Hippasus into the sea, a traitor to all things which numbers, in their marketability, had done for them. Now there is a murder mystery.

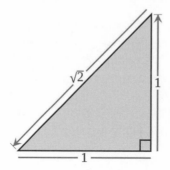

So this first instance of irrationality, proven as it was so easily, caused enormous disruption, blooming just before the death of a mathematical man.

But Hippasus is a stand-in; he's just a guess. History leaves so many guesses, the first proof of the incommensurable unmappable inquiry (situation) where any diagonal crossing the shape of it is unmatchable with any side.

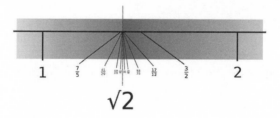

Pythagoras: *All is number.*

And so we conclude, with all respect to the ancient Greeks, that the situation should be that imperfect geometry, that symptom of infinity that contains a hole.

A student posits: I don't know the name of a theory that argues that every single thing in the universe, from the seemingly tiny and fleeting to the horribly compounded, impacted, or intractable, are each exactly equal to each in their irrationality, something like an "irrationality constant" . . .

1.4

On Plato's door: *Let no one enter who does not know geometry.*

You may find the story line difficult to trace. Never looping back to make a unified trajectory, or, unable to find an origin (0,0), the plot is eventually a florescence, though you may object: This isn't about story at all. Only situations sustain a grotesque and barbed peduncle that floats among so many points. You may say: A story is less a slow-move cactus than something that flowers off the bat and spreads easily, reproduces regularly, a curve with an equation, you know, the sort we're familiar with.

A student asks: How can a situation be written in lines?

A situation is not a story, but does it contain story lines?

Sarah Polley: *When you're in the middle of a story, it isn't a story at all, but only a confusion.*

Can a confusion be approached and understood in the way a painting can be approached?

A painting? Students approach.

E. O. Wilson: *In a purely technical sense, each species of higher organism—beetle, moss, and so forth, is richer in information than a Caravaggio painting, Mozart symphony, or any other great work of art. Consider the typical case of the house mouse,* Mus musculus. *Each of its cells contains four strings of DNA, each of which comprises about a billion nucleotide pairs organized into a hundred thousand structural nucleotide pairs, organized into a hundred thousand structural genes . . . The full information therein, if translated into ordinary-sized printed letters, would just about fill all 15 editions of the* Encyclopaedia Britannica *published since 1768.*

Henri Poincare: *Geometry is not true, it is advantageous.*

Ah, we thought we could make this lovely shape, but it slips like a fetid leftover into an irrationality whose non-repeating infinities won't go away.

Taming or canceling or ignoring all the infinities is called the standard model, or *normalization*.

Pythagoras: *A thought is an idea in transit, which when once released, never can be lured back, nor the spoken word recalled. Nor ever can the overt act be erased. All that thou thinkest, sayest or doest bears perpetual record of itself, enduring for eternity.*

And so the student creates magnitudes, whose entanglements, on paper-like substance and consumed in readerly order, attempt to gloss what we might call "situation A." Given that all situations thwart history, it follows that this AB, BC, CA, etcetera . . . provoke a growing dismay. The Greek word *historia* (ἱστορία) means "inquiry through research, and the writing that comes of it."

1.41

Hippasus, having put a dodecahedron in a sphere, may have broadcast the irrational to his ultimate detriment, but neither has anyone to this day squared a circle.

Irrationality was his official secret. But collapse of the form called for (and his rampant personality failure?) proved how violence behaves proportional to solipsism, and that stories of violence, violent stories, do nothing but beg the question.

Take any situation, halve it into two equal situations, then halve it again, then again into an infinity of finely halved arguments (some call this "reality") and this cannot be *summed up* though the parts move relentlessly, futilely, toward zero. Competing and always equally complex realities may be the only reality (just as there are greater and lesser infinities) and stories gain advantage at the direct expense of situations.

This verbal combat, the smiling one-ups, the subtle growling maneuvers, florescence, the many fractured ways grammar can put others in their places, and finally what that means to be *put in a place* (0,0)—this is the subtle violence of story. But being put in a place is only the ratio of one reality to the infinite circumference of the whole situation, and is itself irrational.

Epictetus's *Enchiridion: Let not your laughter be loud, frequent, or unrestrained.*

Laughter being so pleasantly unsubtle, it might have contributed to the death of Hippasus. Laughing loses the thread, becomes useless and possibly dangerous. These objections compare laughter to cruelty, turning a situation antisocial. But the jostling endemic to the slices of spheres shows comedy more exquisite for how seriously each joke is believed. Has anyone grown murderous from laughing? In masquerade and comedy, the laughter always drowns out bureaucracy, if not attempted tyranny.

A student recalls an argument overheard from the top of the stairs. One-sided, or was it two-, three- or more, the battle seeped into restless sleep. In memory, this incompleteness (an overabundance of overhearing) results in the inability to derive history. Approaching the paradox, we tease the incommensurability of the sides. In ecology, arguments promote infinities through hungers, weapons, hubris, actions, reactions, and of course, climate.

Pythagoras: *Begin thus from the first act, and proceed; and, in conclusion, at the ill which thou hast done, be troubled, and rejoice for the good.*

 A student reconsiders the ponderous agave that sits barren, and then after 20 years, offers one enormous, grotesque, disproportioned, ugly, optimistic, awkward growth—and dies. People ask, "If we prevent it flowering, will it live longer?" Sadly, no. Its not-being-there crumples in ruin, just as a giant squid's empty garment floats to the surface, broken and spent. The giant squid remains unknowable except as a form of death. Both the giant agave and giant squid send their fruiting irrationals as once-last tiny situations on the wave.

Students assess side M, then side Y, which is supposed to be commensurate. The angles between add up, it is shapely after all. But side Q says one thing, slightly off, the situation going haywire. The others compensate their angles. The stories seem incongruent, but never where the proof makes it so. Segments are even. Segments are odd. Both deduced because it's not a triangle, or any familiar polyhedron. It is irrational to listen to everyone. It's irrational to understand them.

Protagoras: *Man is the measure of all things.*

Plato: *What I say is that "just" or "right" means nothing but what is in the interest of the stronger side.*

Rationality, for all its emphasis on the discrete, shows itself in an endless spectacle of put-down, a melodrama of beggar's questions (circular, reasoned) practiced before a private, diminishing audience. In a delusion of inner voices, some punchlines gain celebrity estate, but forfeit unruly time and a messy world, their testimonies rigidifying as the slow boil starts, the water appearing preternaturally calm for a while.

Plato: *Is that which is holy loved by the gods because it's holy or is it holy because it's loved by the gods?*

1.41421

Consider a patch of soil which contains the situation (of everyone burrowed, fleeing, flying, infesting, pollinating, destroying, selling, recreating, parasitically inhabiting, or even just happening upon it), the closer we look, the more crowded the patch, not only with creatures but space inside molecules inside creatures joining and dividing energies until there's nothing living inside the living but mystery moving in all directions. If our gawking could peer even farther, we might glimpse something like fate's un-ponderability, *alogos*, and a cracked mirror.

Pythagoras: *It is difficult to walk at one and the same time many paths of life.*

Like irrationals, we are *incommensurable*, with no common measure. Yet so-called rational choice, the way we might proceed, for example, onward—toward success, toward greater [insert positive value here: worth, popularity]—is prim and paradoxical and in its face we are all equal in failure. Your scheme can never be used to make sense of mine, just as Aristotle cannot be understood in terms of Freud (at least not without laughter). Time goes in a line, they say, and the students ask, *Why?* The dimensions of characters, their tangents, are thus illusory and not just in competing *ipse dixits.*

But in our public *sphere* (disobedient, un-sizeable), ultimately our curiosity is all we have to use like a microscope, a weapon, a shell, a claw, or any biological feature, to gain both nourishment and survival. To plot the public sphere, to approach a situation, requires the listening post, and the painful bloodless comic wound where past and present unhinge. Even the smallest fragment of language passes genetically just as preferences, money, hair color, or luck do, giving advantage or crippling handicap. Demon. Strata. Night amplifies a sudden agora to the ears. A starry field. Define universe U with a set I.

1.414213

A mathematician goes to the street and hears ideas leading to vaporous musings in an unnerving investigation that comforts him in a stolen nap. His fellows have convinced him he's a poor talent, and later he goes to battle and dies of a wound. Or he goes to sea and is drowned for his work. What do the living know about keeping "this" and "that" apart in the maelstrom? If he were a writer and not a mathematician, would he have attempted the same proof?

A set is *closed* if its complement (everything that is not in it) is *open*, but this means we can imagine an open set whose complement is also open, making the first set both open and closed, and therefore *clopen*. Your set is *clopen* if and only if its boundary is empty. Complement: everything that is not in set A. Boundary: everything used (passports, police, awards, agents) to be sure that people from below the penthouse are kept out.

Pythagoras: *The oldest, shortest words "yes" and "no"—are those which require the most thought.*

Hence the once-flowering irrational– the one that refuses to be deduced, with no common unit of measure, a carnival of doubters, impossibly howling. *Clopen* in form and function—and also ripe, infected, a bit swollen, chunky, unassimilable, circus-meager, harried, brain-boggled but unafraid of blooming once and dying—the parts slither and stray, overlap unyieldingly to excerpting. Made finally of precious paper and distributed by hand, a wilder boundary than we can imagine, across the so-called garden wall. It's an eavesdropper's, grave-robber's project, publicly assembling taxonomic monsters from long-buried situations just as giant squid are only known for being unknowable.

A giant squid's life proceeds without human witness, in the unprecedented layers beyond the outer legal system. Only later, its anatomy parceled when it washes up too late, color drained, eye bigger than previously thought, from finding its obscure meals and running obscure errands. Gliding obscurely in the obscure rain, obscure in the thermal currents, its arguments and situations dispersed in sudden inky clouds.

1.4142135

Cats are shapely, half-dead, and adorn the *agora* with struts, shrugs, their lounging, and love-fights. As interference breaks through interface, arguers stand on shoulders, squabbling in rough voices to ascend conundrums and "speak up," the hard-of-being-heard sulking offstage, ready to shoot. Anointed experts step in to moderate, other authorities accuse and refute, prove by numbers, take up celebrity. Rebels erase authority. Horses stampede from the barn. Then the space must be trucked off, or the accumulation desisted. Riot police. Invitation to "dialogue" that is nothing but privileged personalities in bare disguise. An *agon* unrelents, pulls up the tent corner stakes until the confused geometry calms.

Aristoxenus: *Whenever he heard a person who was making use of his symbols, he immediately took him into his circle, and made him a friend.*

The public space fills with actors, "real people," and birds crossing a crowd of best-guesses. The multitude is the richness, not its demise. An argument: a moment of crystalized wonder.

Students examine the agave: its inflorescent afterlife and decomposition. The death that seeds and signals the finale. Can you stop an agave from *flowering*

and keep it from dying
by cutting off its stalk?
No
the pro
cess that causes the plan
t to flow
er also kills
the plan
t

1.41421356

Student: Or was he in exile? The secret that Hippasus stole and not for sharing?

Another student: The square root of two exists, it's a line on a paper.

Student: But it also doesn't exist, because its expression is impossible.

Another student: So if we can't express, we don't exist?

Ralph Waldo Emerson: *Speak what you think now in hard words, and tomorrow speak what tomorrow thinks in hard words again, though it contradict everything you said to-day.—"Ah, so you shall be sure to be misunderstood."*

So even expressive silence provides literary proof, just as a giant squid's stomach bisects its brain. The leg a tentacle where eggs circulate. Three hearts power up astonishing escapes. Nothing familiar, just extrapolations from corpses and forms. Jaw hole of razors; "We can only guess," the experts recoil, "what this might be for!" The squid gives birth from her leg, and only once, before she sails dead to the floor. Who would accept this monster? Yet we are encouraged to watch Masai giraffes on the zoo's giraffe-cam without leaving the couch. "If the giraffes are not in their enclosure, it might be a nice day."

Aristotle: *So poetry is something more philosophical and more worthy of serious attention than history.*

1.414213562

The funny part is that Pythagoras never wrote anything in his lifetime, nor did his contemporaries write about him. What?

We don't know what he *factually* said, did, or thought. We do not know if he was even a mathematician, as there is no mention of mathematics in any early writings about him or his followers. The first accounts, written 150 or so years after he died, disagree extensively about his life. Only in the 4–5th centuries BCE do hagiographies call him a divine being, positioning him as the origin of Plato's philosophy. That his teachings were largely secret justified the lack of written texts, and allowed for the many buried forgeries "found" centuries later.

Thus a situation; inquiry tangles. One says Pythagoras ate some meat. Another: he was strictly vegetarian. Eudoxus: "he not only abstained from animal food but would not come near butchers or hunters." Aristotle: "the Pythagoreans refrain from eating the womb and the heart, the sea anemone, and some other things, but use all other animal food." Many say Pythagoras influenced Plato's metaphysics. Plato never mentions him. Aristotle only calls them the "so-called Pythagoreans," who may have known of limiters and unlimiteds, though this is likely a reference to Hippasus. In Aristotle's missing treatise on these so-called Pythagoreans, he may have described Pythagoras as a miracle-worker with a golden leg, who bit a snake and was able to be in two places at once. Aristotle says he prohibited eating beans, but Aristoxenus says "he valued beans most of all vegetables, since they were laxative."

A student, unrelenting (like it's the last thing she'll ever do): So if inquiries are infinite, isn't the only possible story irrational?

Each is right. They are all wrong. The towering peduncle may be magnificent but its appearance equals its death, or just the transfer of stored nourishment to the act of seeding. The flowering agave gives people soap, pens, awls, paper, needles, sugar, string, medicine, rope, tequila, fiber, and a variety of food and drink.

Empedocles, on Pythagoras: *A man who possessed the greatest wealth of intelligence!*

Heraclitus: *King of the Charlatans!*

GLANCING BACKWARD

—

> "on the sinking ark, look for the elephants first
> and drop them overboard before anyone else."
> *Vilfredo Pereto*

We also say earth is "like a person"
a hypothesis, another goddess
hold up, Gaia, it will only take a minute (more or less)
in geothermal time
—to wake—any second now!
to tally what is spent and not repaid—
a kind of carbon song-cycle on a televised talent contest.

Emancipation says, *release from the hand*—
all who can fly
all who can run
and crawl, worms, into unchewed boreal leaf-litter—
where bees can't follow disoriented Orpheus,
his self-serving crooning, his pretend
not-knowing where madness lies
between flower and fruit.

And from whatever self-proclaimed God's fat fist
—*ex manus capere*—

do we expect release,
when mighty Zeus sits hoarding bullion and fresh-water,
blocking the clean-up crew from his trashed hotel room.
And tired Atlas drops the ball, to chase imaginary dragons
rather than uphold Minnie, Beulah, and Karen—
elephant plaintiffs before the High Court
seeking release from the daily, greedy circus—
Judge: "Their petition is wholly frivolous."

And while pending appeal, Beulah falls on her side
at the Big E fair in Springfield, Mass and dies.
Killed by those who say they love animals
(so many of us love animals)
another empire killed by those who pretend to defend it.
What simple rule did we ignore?
What moment past the tipping point?
Which magic word?

NOTES

Earlier versions of chapters from *Personhood* appeared in the following books and journals: *Animal Comics: Multispecies Storyworlds in Graphic Narratives* (London: Bloomsbury Academic, 2017), *Conjunctions, Passages North, Portland Review*, and *Review of Contemporary Fiction*.

QUOTATIONS FROM "HAPPY/THAT YOU HAVE THE BODY (THE MIRROR TEST): The "habeas corpus" definition is from *WEX Legal Dictionary*. Mr. Wise, Mr. Manning, and court quotations appear in legal briefs from the Nonhuman Rights Project. The Richard Cupp quotation is from the *Washington Post* (Aug. 13, 2018). Quotations from Dr. Diana Reiss, used by permission. The Pakistan High Court quotation is taken from *Judgment Sheet in the Islamabad High Court, Islamabad (Judicial Department) W.P., No. 1155/2019*. The *Mahavibhasa* quotation is from *Unfortunate Destiny: Animals in the Indian Buddhist Imagination*, by Reiko Ohnuma (New York: Oxford University Press, 2017).

IN LIBERTY/TREES: "Like Trees/Walking" refers to an amazing novel by Ravi Howard.

QUOTATIONS FROM "THE HEALTH OF MY STREAM": Zhuangzi quotations are from *The Complete Works of Zhuangzi*, translated by Burton Watson (New York: Columbia University Press, 2013). "In the High Courts of Uttarakhand at Nainital" is extracted from a legal brief.

QUOTATIONS FROM "IRRATIONAL/SITUATION": E. O. Wilson quotation, from *Nature Revealed: Selected Writings, 1949-2006* (Baltimore: Johns Hopkins University Press, 2006).

PHOTO AND IMAGE CREDITS: *Bird Photos*, courtesy of Brian Jones/Foster Parrots; *photo of Happy with X*, courtesy of Joshua M. Plotnik, Frans B. M. de Waal, and Diana Reiss; *photo of painting elephant*, courtesy of Thalia Field; *artwork by Bridget Brewer in "True Crime/Nature Fakers,"* courtesy of the artist and the Bates College German Department; *stream photo in "The Health of My Stream,"* courtesy of Thalia Field; *photo of Beulah the elephant on her side*, courtesy of Jill Alibrandi.